The Debt to Pleasure

The Debt to Pleasure

A Novel

John Lanchester

M&S

Canadian Cataloguing in Publication Data

Lanchester, John
 The debt to pleasure

ISBN 0-7710-4585-9

I. Title.

PR6062.A4863D43 1996   823'.914   C95-933196-4

Published in the United States of America by
Henry Holt and Company, Inc., New York, and
in the United Kingdom by Picador, an imprint
of Macmillan General Books, London.

Printed and bound in the U.S.A. on acid-free paper

Designed by Lucy Albanese
Illustrations by Peter Campbell

McClelland & Stewart Inc.
The Canadian Publishers
481 University Avenue
Toronto, Ontario
M5G 2E9

1 2 3 4 5   00 99 98 97 96

IN MEMORY OF MY FATHER

My German engineer was very argumentative and tiresome. He wouldn't admit that it was certain that there was not a rhinoceros in the room.

—Bertrand Russell,
letter to Ottoline Morrell

Preface,
Acknowledgment,
and a Note on Structure

This is not a conventional cookbook. Though I should straightaway attach a disclaimer to my disclaimer and say that I have nothing but the highest regard for the traditional collection of recipes, arranged by ingredient under broad, usually geographical categories. One of the charms of the genre is that it places an admirably high premium on accuracy. The omission of a single word or a single instruction can inflict a humiliating fiasco on the unsuspecting home cook. Which of us has not completed a recipe to the letter, only to look down and see, lying unused by the side of the sauté pan, a recriminatory pile of chopped onions? One early disaster of my brother's, making a doomed attempt to impress some hapless love object, was occasioned by the absence of the small word "plucked"—he removed from the oven a roasted but full-fledged pheasant, terrible in its hot sarcophagus of feathers.

The classic cookbook borrows features from the otherwise radically opposed genres of encyclopedia and confession. On the one hand, the world categorized, diagnosed, defined, explained, alphabeticized; on the other, the self laid bare, all quirks and anecdotes and personal history. All contributions to the form belong on a continuum with *Larousse Gastronomique* at one end and at the other . . . well, perhaps I can leave that to the reader's imagination. One could name here any of the works of which my Provençal (English) neighbor (now dead) used to say: "I *love* cookbooks—d'you know, I read them like *novels!*"

But as I say, this is not a conventional cookbook. The presiding spirit of this work, and the primary influence on it, is the nineteenth-century culino-philosophico-autobiographical volume *La Physiologie du Goût* by the judge, soldier, violinist, language teacher, gourmand, and philosopher Jean-Anthelme Brillat-Savarin, who ranks with the Marquis de Sade as one of the two great oppositional minds of the period. Brillat-Savarin, after narrowly escaping death during the French Revolution ("the most surprising thing that has hitherto happened in the world," according to Burke), was mayor of Belley, and a judge on the post-revolutionary supreme court in Paris. His sisters would stay in bed for three months of the year, building up strength for his annual visit. His best-known remark is probably the aphorism "Tell me what you eat and I'll tell you who you are," though I personally have always preferred his summing up of a lifetime's eating: "I have drawn the following inference, that the limits to pleasure are as yet neither known nor fixed." The original cheese named after Brillat-Savarin suffered a change of ownership in the early 1970s and is now made by Fromageries de Pansey in the Champagne area; contemporary editions of the cheese strike many observers as disappointingly underpowered.

I must also acknowledge a more immediate inspiration. Over the years, many people have pleaded with me to commit to paper my thoughts on the subject of food. Indeed the words "Why don't you write a book about it?," uttered in an admittedly wide variety of tones and inflections, have come to possess something of the quality of a mantra—one tending to be provoked by a disquisition of mine on, for instance, the composition of an authoritative *cassoulet,* or Victorian techniques for baking hedgehogs in clay. I have always had a certain resistance to the notion of publishing my own *physiologie du goût,* on the grounds that I did not want to distract attention from my artistic work in other media. Recently, however, I have come to believe that no harm will accrue from bringing before the public something which—while not composed casually or "with the left hand"—nonetheless claims to be nothing more than a shaving from the master's workbench.

This work came to be written—this long-toyed-with suggestion suddenly crystallized into factuality—principally thanks to my young collaborator, Laura Tavistock. She is by far the most charming, most persuasive, and most recent of those who have felt themselves urged to urge me to this project. If I have not dedicated this book to her that is because, at this stage of the joint enterprise on which Ms. Tavistock and I are engaged, such a gesture might seem (to use a phrase of hers) "a bit previous."

I have falsified one or two proper names and place names. For instance, "Mary-Theresa" and "Mitthaug" are close approximations rather than mean and mere identicalities. (Does that word exist? It does now.) St-Eustache is not St-Eustache. The Hotel Splendide is not the Hotel Splendide.

About the architecture of this book. Its organization is based on the times and places of its composition. In the late middle of summer I decided to take a short holiday and travel southward through France, which is, as the reader will learn, my spiritual (and for a portion of the year, actual) homeland. I resolved that I would jot down my thoughts on the subject of food as I went, taking my cue from the places and events around me as well as from my own memories, dreams, reflections, the whole simmering together, synergistically exchanging savors and essences like some ideal *daube.* This will, I hope, give the book a serendipitous, ambulatory, and yet progressive structure. One consequence of the decision to take this course is that I am, as I set down these sentences, in the unusual position of writing my preface before the rest of my narrative. We are all familiar with the after-the-fact tone—weary, self-justificatory, aggrieved, apologetic—shared by ship captains appearing before boards of inquiry to explain how they came to run their vessels aground, and by authors composing forewords.

Finally: I have decided that, wherever possible, the primary vehicle for the transmission of my culinary reflections will be the menu. These menus shall be arranged seasonally. It seems to me that the menu lies close to the heart of the human impulse to order, to beauty, to pattern. It draws on the original chthonic upwelling that underlies all art. A menu can embody the anthropology of a culture or the psychology of an individual; it can be a biography, a cultural history, a lexicon; it speaks to the sociology, psychology, and biology of its creator and its audience, and of course to their geographical location; it can be a way of knowledge, a path, an inspiration, a Tao, an ordering, a shaping, a manifestation, a talisman, an injunction, a memory, a fantasy, a consolation, an allusion, an illusion, an evasion, an assertion, a seduction, a prayer, a summoning, an incantation murmured under the breath as the torchlights sink lower and the forest looms taller and the wolves howl louder and the fire prepares for its submission to the encroaching dark.

I'm not sure that this would be *my* choice for a honeymoon hotel. The gulls outside my window are louder than motorcycles.

Tarquin Winot
Hotel Splendide, Portsmouth

· Winter ·

Two Menus

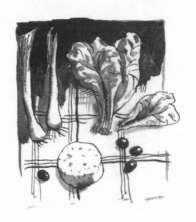

A Winter Menu

Winston Churchill was fond of saying that the Chinese ideogram for "crisis" is composed of the two characters which separately mean "danger" and "opportunity."

Winter presents the cook with a similar combination of threat and chance. It is, perhaps, winter which is responsible for a certain brutalization of the British national palate, and a concomitant affection for riotous sweet-and-sour combinations, aggressive pickles, pungent sauces, and ketchups. More on this later. But the threat of winter is also, put simply, that of an overreliance on stodge. Northern European readers will need no further elaboration: the "stodge" term, the stodge concept, covers a familiar universe of inept nursery food, hostile saturated fats, and intentful carbohydrates. (There is a sinister genius in the very *name* Brown Windsor Soup.) It is a style of cooking which has attained its apotheosis in England's public schools, and though I myself was spared the horrors of such an education—my parents, correctly judging my nature to be too fine-grained and sensitive, employed a succession of private tutors—I have vivid memories of my one or two visits to my brother during his incarceration in various gulags.

I remember the last of these safaris with particular clarity. I was eleven years old. My brother, then seventeen and on the brink of his final expulsion, was resident in a boarding school my father described as "towards the top of the second division." I think my parents had gone to the school in an attempt to persuade the headmaster not to expel Bartholomew, or perhaps he had won some dreary school art award. In any case, we were "given the tour." One of its most impressing features was the dormitory in which my brother slept. This was heated by a single knobbly metal pipe, painted black in ignorance of the laws of physics or in a conscious attempt to defy them, or in a deliberate effort to make the room even colder. The pipe had no effect whatsoever on the ambient temperature—Bartholomew and the nineteen other boys in the dormitory would regularly wake to find a generous layer of ice on the inside of the windows—but was itself so hot that any skin contact resulted instantaneously in severe burns. The fact that school-uniform socks were mandatorily only of ankle length meant that the possibility of flesh-to-pipe contact was formidably high, so that (according to Bartholomew) the smell of burnt epidermis was a familiar feature of school life.

We had been invited to lunch. A long, low, paneled room, perfectly decent architecturally, housed a dozen trestle tables, each of which held what seemed to be an impossibly large number of noisy boys. The walls were hung with bad sludge-colored paintings of defunct headmasters, a procession interrupted only by the most recent portrait, which was a large black-and-white photograph of a handsome sadist in an ermine-rimmed MA gown; and the one before it, which suggested either that the artist was a tragicomically inept doctrinaire cubist, or that Mr. R. B. Fenner-Crossway MA was in reality a dyspeptic pattern of mauve rhomboids. A gong was struck as we entered; the boys stood in a prurient scrutinizing silence as my parents and I, attached to a straggling procession of staff members, progressed the length of the hall to the high table, set laterally across the room. My brother was embarrassedly in tow. I could feel sweat behind my knees. A hulking Aryan prefect figure, an obvious thug, bully, and teacher's favorite, spoke words of Latin benediction into the hush.

We then sat down to a meal which Dante would have hesitated to invent. I was seated opposite my parents, between a spherical house-matron and a silent French *assistant.* The first course was a soup in which pieces of undisguised and unabashed gristle floated in a mud-colored sauce whose texture and temperature were powerfully reminiscent of mucus. Then a steaming vat was placed in the middle of the table, where the jowly, watch-chained headmaster presided. He plunged his serving arm into the vessel and emerged with a ladleful of hot food, steaming like fresh horse dung on a cold morning. For a heady moment I thought I was going to be sick. A plate of *soi-disant* cottage pie—the mince gray, the potato beige—was set in front of me.

"The boys call this 'mystery meat,'" confided the matron happily. I felt the *assistant* flinch. Other than that I don't remember (I can't imagine) what we talked about, and over the rest of the meal—as Swinburne's biographer remarked, *à propos* an occasion when his subject had misbehaved during a lecture on the subject of Roman sewage systems—"the Muse of history must draw her veil."

There is an erotics of dislike. It can be (I am indebted to a young friend for the helpful phrase) "a physical thing." Roland Barthes observes somewhere that the meaning of any list of likes and dislikes is to be found in its assertion of the fact that each of us has a body, and that this body is different from everybody else's. This is tosh. The real meaning of our dislikes is that they define us by separating us from what is outside us; they separate the self from the world in a way that mere banal liking cannot do. ("Gourmandism is an act of judgment, by which we give preference to those things which are agreeable to our taste over those which are not."—Brillat-Savarin) To like some-

6

thing is to want to ingest it, and in that sense is to submit to the world. To like something is to succumb, in a small but contentful way, to death. But dislike hardens the perimeter between the self and the world, and brings a clarity to the object isolated in its light. Any dislike is in some measure a triumph of definition, distinction, and discrimination—a triumph of life.

I am not exaggerating when I say that this visit to my brother at St. Botolph's (not its real name) was a defining moment in my development. The combination of human, aesthetic, and culinary banality formed a negative revelation of great power, and hardened the already burgeoning suspicion that my artist's nature isolated and separated me from my alleged fellowmen. France rather than England, art rather than society, separation rather than immersion, doubt and exile rather than yeomanly certainty, *gigot à quarante gousses d'ail* rather than roast lamb with mint sauce. "Two roads diverged in a wood, and I—I took the one less traveled by / And that has made all the" (important word coming up) "difference."

This might seem a lot of biographical significance to attribute to a single bad experience with a shepherd's pie. (I have sometimes tried to establish a distinction between cottage pie, made with beef leftovers, and shepherd's pie, made with lamb, but it doesn't seem to have caught on so I have abandoned it. They order these things differently in France.) Nevertheless I hope I have made my point about the importance of the cook's maintaining a proactive stance vis-à-vis the problem of the winter diet.

Winter should be seen as an opportunity for the cook to demonstrate, through the culinary arts, his mastery of balance and harmony and his oneness with the seasons; to express the deep concordances of his own and nature's rhythms. The tastebuds should be titillated, flirted with, provoked. The following menu is an example of how this may be done. The flavors in it possess a certain quality of intensity suitable for those months of the year when one's tastebuds feel swaddled.

> *Blinis with Sour Cream and Caviar*
> *Irish Stew*
> *Queen of Puddings*

Of the many extant batter, pancake, and waffle dishes—*crèpes* and *galettes*, Swedish *krumkakor, sockerstruvor*, and *plättar*, Finnish *tattoriblinit*, generic Scandinavian *äggvåffla*, Italian *brigidini*, Belgian *gaufrettes*, Polish *nalesniki*, Yorkshire pudding—blinis are my personal favorite. The distinguishing characteristics of the blini, as a member of the happy family of pancakes, is that it is thick (as opposed to thin), nonfolding (as opposed to folding), and raised with yeast (as opposed to bicarbonate of soda); it is Russian; and like the Breton sarrasin pancake, it is made of buckwheat (as opposed to plain flour). Buckwheat is not a grass, and therefore not a cereal, and therefore does not fall under the protection of the goddess Ceres, the Roman deity who presided over agriculture. On her feast day, in a strangely evocative ceremony, foxes with their tails on fire were let loose in the Circus Maximus; nobody knows why. The Greek equivalent of Ceres was the goddess Demeter, mother of Persephone. It was in Demeter's honor that the Eleusinian mysteries were held, a legacy of the occasion when she was forced to reveal her divinity in order to explain why she was holding King Celeus's baby in the fire—no doubt a genuinely embarrassing and difficult to explain moment, even for a goddess.

Blinis. Sift 4 oz. buckwheat flour, mix with ½ oz. yeast (dissolved in warm water) and ¼ pint warm milk, leave for fifteen minutes. Mix 4 oz. flour with ½ pint milk, add 2 egg yolks, 1 tsp. sugar, 1 tbs. melted butter and a pinch of salt, whisk the two blends together. Leave for an hour. Add 2 whisked egg whites. Right. Now heat a heavy cast-iron frying pan of the type known in both classical languages as a *placenta*—which is, as everybody knows, not at all the same thing as the caul or wrapping in which the fetus lives when it is inside the womb. To be born in the caul, as I was, is a traditional indication of good luck, conferring second sight and immunity from death by drowning; preserved cauls used to attract a premium price from superstitious sailors. Freud was born in the caul, as was the hero of his favorite novel, David Copperfield. Sometimes, if there is more than one sibling in the family, one of them born in the caul and the other not, the obvious difference between them in terms of luck, charm, and talent can be woundingly great, and the fact of one of them having been born in the caul can cause intense jealousy and anger, particularly when that gift is accompanied by other personal

9

and artistic distinctions. But one must remember that while it is disagreeable to be on the receiving end of such emotions it is of course far more degrading to be the person who experiences them. To claim that one's five-year-old brother pushed one out of a treehouse, for instance, and caused one to break one's arm, when in fact one fell in the course of trying to climb higher up the tree in order to gain a vantage from which one could spy into the nanny's room, is a despicable way of retaliating for that younger brother's having charmed the nanny by capturing her likeness with five confident strokes of finger paint and then shyly handing the artwork to her with a little dedicatory poem (This is for you, Mary-T / Because you are the one for me) written across the top in yellow crayon.

When smoke starts to rise out of the pan add the batter in assured dollops, bearing in mind that each little dollop is to become a blini when it grows up, and that the quantities given here are sufficient for six. Turn them over when bubbles appear on top.

Serve the pancakes with sour cream and caviar. Sour cream is completely straightforward and if you need any advice or guidance about it then, for you, I feel only pity. Caviar, the cleaned and salted roe of the sturgeon, is a little more complicated. The surprisingly un-German, Wisconsin-born sociologist Thorstein Veblen formulated something he called "the scarcity theory of value," to argue that objects increase in value in direct proportion to their perceived rarity rather than their intrinsic merit or interest. In other words, if Marmite was as hard to come by as caviar, would it be as highly prized? (Of course, there is an experimentally determinable answer to this, because we know that among British expatriate communities commodities such as Marmite and baked beans have virtually the status of bankable currency. When my brother was living near Arles he once, in the course of a game of poker with an actor who had retired to run a shop targeting nostalgic Englishpeople, won a year's supply of chocolate digestive biscuits. In the ensuing twelve months he put on ten pounds which he was never to lose.) Lurking in this idea is the question of whether or not caviar is—not to put too fine a point on it—"worth it." All I can say in response to that is to point to the magic of the sturgeon, producer of these delicate exotic rare expensive eggs, and one of the oldest animals on the planet, in existence in something closely resembling its current form for about two hundred million years. The fish grows to twelve feet in length, and has a snout with which it roots for food underneath the sea bed; when you eat caviar you are partaking of this mysterious juxtaposition of the exquisite and the atavistic. And spending a lot of money into the bargain, of course. Caviar is graded according to the size of its grains, which in turn vary according to the size of the fish from which they are taken: *beluga* being the biggest, then *ossetra,* then *sevruga; ossetra,* whose eggs span the spectrum of colors from dirty battleship to occluded sunflower, is my roe of choice. Much of the highest grade caviar carries the designation *malassol,* which means "lightly salted."

The process by which the correct level of salting is applied to Volga caviar is insufficiently well known. The master taster—a rough-and-ready seeming fellow he is likely to be, too, with a knit cap on his head, a gleam in his eye, and a dagger in his boot—takes a single egg into his mouth and rolls it around his palate. By applying his almost mystically fine amalgam of experience and talent, he straightaway knows how much salt to add to the sturgeon's naked roe. The consequences of any inaccuracy are disastrous, gastronomically and economically (hence the dagger). There are analogies with the way in which an artist—I am not thinking only of myself—can judge the quality of a work of art with a rapidity that appears instantaneous, as if the acts of visual apprehension and of critical estimation are simultaneous, or even as if the judgment infinitesimally precedes the encounter with the artwork, as in one of the paradoxes of quantum physics, or as in a dream one constructs an elaborate narrative, expanding confidently across time and space and involving many fragmentations of person and object—a deceased relative who is also a tuba, an airplane flight to Argentina which is also a memory of one's first sexual experience, a misfiring revolver which is also a wig—before coming to a terrifying climax with the noise of the siren ringing out across London to announce the imminent outbreak of nuclear war, a sound which resolves itself into the banal but infinitely reassuring domestic event that somehow contained within it the whole of the preceding story: the happy jangling of an alarm clock, or the arrival at the front door of one's favorite postman, carrying an inconveniently large parcel.

Caviar is sometimes eaten by chess players as a way of rapidly consuming a considerable quantity of easily digestible protein, without any of the stupefying effects of a bona fide meal. It is an excellent cold weather food. It is not available on cross-channel ferries such as this one, though in many respects it would be an ideal mid-journey picnic. There is, however, a deliriously vulgar "caviar bar" at Heathrow Terminal Four, just to the right of the miniature Harrods.

The chemistry of yeast, incidentally, has not yet been entirely deciphered by scientists. I take this to be a reminder that there are still some mysteries left, some corners and crevices of the universe which are still opaque to us. For me, this dish, perhaps because of its connection or nonconnection with Demeter (for, as Buddhism teaches us, nonconnection can be a higher form of connection), is irrevocably bound up with the idea of mystery. I must confess to taking some pleasure from the fact that if it is not possible to diminish the magic of rising yeast then perhaps there are one or two corners of poetry left in a world that at times seems depleted and diminished by explanation. I myself have always disliked being called a "genius." It is fascinating to notice how quick people have been to intuit this aversion and avoid using the term.

With liberal additions of sour cream and caviar the above recipe—I prefer the old-fashioned spelling "receipt," but it was pointed out to me that "if you call it that nobody will have a f***ing clue what you're talking about"—represents adequate quantities for six people as a starter, providing several blinis each. Perhaps I have already said that. It is only sensible to construct an entire meal out of blinis if one is planning to spend the rest of the day out on the *taiga,* boasting about women and shooting bears.

Irish stew is uncomplicated, though none the less tasty for that. It is forever associated in my mind (my heart, my palate) with my Cork-born, Skibbereen-raised nanny, Mary-Theresa. She was one of the few fixed points of a childhood that was for its first decade or so distinctly itinerant. My father's business interests kept him on the move; my mother's former profession—the stage—had given her a taste for travel and the sensation of movement. She liked to live not so much out of suitcases as out of trunks, creating a home that at the same time contained within it the knowledge that this was the *illusion* of home, a stage set or theatrical redescription of safety and embowering domesticity; her wall-hung carpets and portable bibelots (a lacquered Chinese screen, a lean, malignly upright Egyptian cat made of onyx) were a way of saying "Let's pretend." She would, I think, have preferred to regard motherhood as merely another feat of impersonation; but it was as if an intermittently amusing cameo part had gruelingly protracted itself, and what was intended to be an experimental production (King Lear as a senile brewery magnate, Cordelia on rollerskates) had turned into an inadvertent *Mousetrap,* with my mother stuck in a frumpy role she had only taken on in the first place as a favor to the hard-pressed director. To put it another way, she treated parenthood as analogous to the parts forced on an actor past his prime or of eccentric physique who has been obliged to specialize in "characters." She was ironic, distracted, and self-pitying, with a way of implying that, now that the best things in life were over, she would take on *this* role. She would check one's fingernails or take one to the circus with the air of someone bravely concealing an unfavorable medical prognosis: the children must never know! But she also had a public mode in which she played at being a mother in the way that a very *very* distinguished actress, caught overnight in the Australian outback (train derailed by dead wallaby or flash flood), is forced to put up at a tiny settlement where, she is half-appalled and half-charmed to discover, the feisty pioneers have been preparing for weeks to put on, this very same evening, under wind-powered electric lights, a production of *Hamlet.* Discovering the identity of their newcomer (via a blurred photograph in a torn-out magazine clipping brandished by a stammering admirer) the locals insist that she take a, no *the,* starring role; she prettily demurs; they anguishedly insist; she becomingly surrenders, on the condition that she play the smallest and least likely of roles—the gravedigger, say. And gives a performance which, decades later, the descendants of the original cast still sometimes discuss as they rock on their porches to watch the only train of the day pass silhouetted against the huge ochres and impossibly elongated shadows of the desert sunset . . . that was the spirit in which my mother "did" being a mother. To be her child during these public episodes was to be uplifted, irradiated, fortune's darling. But if this, as has recently been observed to me, "makes her sound like a total nightmare," then I am omitting the way in which one was encouraged to collude in her role-playing, and was also allowed great freedom of maneuver by it. With a part of oneself conscripted to act the other role in whatever production she was undertaking—duet or ensemble, Brecht or Pinter, Ibsen or Stoppard or Aeschylus—a considerable amount of one's emotional space was left vacant, thanks to her essential and liberating lack of interest.

So travel and the condition of itinerancy did not bother my mother, which is just as well as it was a fundamental aspect of my father's business activities. I therefore had a mobile childhood in which the rites of passage were geographically as well as temporally distinct. Thus I have somewhere a maltreated red leather photograph album with a picture in it of me holding my mother's hand; I am looking into the camera with an air of suppressed triumph as I proudly model my first-ever pair of long trousers. The proliferation of out-of-focus yacht masts in the background gives less of a clue than it should: Cowes? Portofino? East Looe? Another picture shows a view from the outside of the high-windowed, difficult-to-heat ground-floor flat in Bayswater (still in my possession) where my father provided the first external reflection of the inner vocational light I felt glimmering within me: he picked up a watercolor I had made that afternoon (hothouse mimosa and dried lavender in a glass jar) and said, "D'you know, I think the lad's got something." That memory brings with it the smell of the parquet flooring which, on otherwise unoccupied afternoons, I used to dig up with my fingers, less for the pleasure of vandalism than for the heady and magically comforting odor of the gummy resin that bound the oblong blocks in place. When you'd dug up a tile, however carefully you put it back, it somehow never looked the same again. That parquet pattern, arranged so that the four-tile squares were aligned with the corners of the room in the shape of a squat diamond, had an air of interpretability, of cabalistic significance; as if, gazed at long enough or hard enough, it would be bound eventually to yield a meaning, a clue. Or our flat in Paris, off the rue d'Assas in the 6ème, still vivid to me as the location for my first encounter with the death of a pet: a hamster called Hercule who had been placed in my brother's charge by our sinister concierge's grandson during their August visit to relatives in Normandy. My father wore a black tie when he went downstairs to break the news.

In these early years Mary-Theresa was a constant presence, in the first instance as a nanny and subsequently as a *bonne* or maid-of-all-work. Although cooking was not central to her function in the household, she would venture into the kitchen on those not infrequent occasions when whoever was employed to be our cook—a Dostoevskian procession of knaves, dreamers, drunkards, visionaries, bores, and frauds, every man his own light, every man his own bushel—was absent; though she *had* left our employ by the most memorable of these occasions, the time when Mitthaug, our counterstereotypically garrulous and optimistic Norwegian cook with a special talent for pickling, failed to arrive in time to make the necessary preparations for an important dinner party because (as it turned out) he had been run over by a train.

In these circumstances Mary-Theresa would, with an attractive air of ceremonial determination, don the blue-fringed apron she kept for specifically this emergency, and advance purposefully into the kitchen to emerge later with one of the dishes which, after extensive intrafamilial debates, she had been trained to cook: fish pie, omelette, roast chicken, and steak and kidney pudding; or alternatively she would prepare her *spécialité,* Irish stew. As a result the aroma of this last dish became something of a unifying theme in the disparate locations of my upbringing, a binding agent whose action in coalescing these various locales into a consistent, individuated, remembered narrative— into my story—is, I would propose, not unlike the binding action supplied in various recipes by cream, butter, flour, arrowroot, *beurre manié,* blood, ground almonds (a traditional English expedient, not to be despised), or, as in the recipe I am about to give, by the more dissolvable of two different kinds of potato. When Mary-Theresa had to be dismissed it was perhaps the smell and flavor of this dish that I missed most.

Assemble your ingredients. It should be admitted that authorities differ as to which cut of meat to use in this dish. I have in my time read three sources who respectively prefer "boned lamb shanks or leftover lamb roast," "middle end of neck of lamb," and "best end of neck lamb chops." My own view is that any of these cuts is acceptable in what is basically a peasant dish (a comment on its history, not its flavor). Mutton is of course more flavorsome than lamb, although it has become virtually impossible to obtain. There used to be a butcher who sold mutton not far from our house in Norfolk, but he died. As for the preference expressed by some people for boned lamb in an Irish stew, I can only say that Mary-Theresa used to insist on the osseous variation, with its extra flavor as well as the beguiling hint of gelatinousness provided by the marrow. Three pounds of lamb: scrag or middle of neck, or shank, ideally with the bone still in. One and a half pounds of firm-fleshed potatoes: Bishop or Pentland Javelin if using British varieties, otherwise interrogate your grocer. One and a half pounds of floury potatoes, intended to dissolve in the manner alluded to above. In Britain: Maris Piper or King Edward. Or ask. There used to be a very good grocer at the corner of rue Cassette and rue Chevalier in the 6ème, but I don't suppose he's there anymore. (Science has not given us a full account of the difference between floury and waxy potatoes. If the reader is having a problem identifying to what category his potato belongs, he should drop it into a solution containing one part salt to eleven parts water: floury potatoes sink.) One and a half pounds of sliced onions. A selection of herbs to taste—oregano, a bay leaf, thyme, marjoram. If using dry varieties—about two teaspoons. Salt. Trim the lamb into cutlets and procure a casserole that's just big enough. Peel the potatoes and slice them thickly. Layer the ingredients as follows: layer hard potatoes; layer onions; layer lamb; layer soft potatoes; layer onions; layer lamb; repeat as necessary and finish with a thick layer of all remaining potatoes. Sprinkle each layer with salt and herbs. You will of course not be able to do that if you have been following this recipe without reading it through in advance. Let that be a lesson to you. Add cold water down the interstices of meat and vegetables until it insinuates up to the top. Put a lid on it. Cook for three hours in an oven at gas mark two. You will find that the soft potatoes have dissolved into the cooking liquid. Serves six trencherpersons. The ideological purity of this recipe is very moving.

The broad philosophical distinction between types of stew is between preparations that involve an initial cooking of some kind—frying or sautéing or whatever it may be—and those that do not. Irish stew is the paladin of the latter type of stew; other members of the family include the Lancashire Hot Pot, which is distinguishable from Irish stew only by the optional inclusion of kidneys and the fact that in the latter stages of cooking the British version of the dish is browned with the lid off. The similarity between the two dishes testifies to the close cultural affinities between Lancashire and Ireland; it was in Manchester that my father "discovered" Mary-Theresa working, as he put it, "in a blacking factory"—in reality through a business colleague who had hired her in advance of his wife's parturition, going so far as to employ a private detective to check her references, and then dismissing her when it turned out that his spouse was undergoing a phantom pregnancy. Boiled mutton is a cousin to these preparations, and an underrated dish in its own right, being especially good when eaten with its time-honored accompaniment ("It gives an epicure the vapours / To eat boiled mutton without capers"—Ogden Nash); one should also take into account the hearty, Germano-Alsatian dish *backenoff,* made with mutton, pork, beef, and potatoes; soothing *blanquette de veau,* exempted from initial browning but thickened by cream at the last moment; and of course the twin classic *daubes à la Provençale* and *à l'Avignonnaise.* In France, indeed, the generic name for this type of stew—cooked from cold—is *daube,* after the *daubière,* a pot with a narrow neck and a bulging swollen middle reminiscent of the Buddha's stomach.

In the other kind of stew, whose phylum might well be the sauté or braise, the ingredients are subjected to an initial cooking at high temperature, in order to promote the processes of thickening and binding (where flour or another such agent is used) and also to encourage a preliminary exchange of flavors. As Huckleberry Finn puts it: "In a barrel of odds and ends it is different; things get mixed up, and the juice kind of swaps around, and things go better." Notice that the initial cooking does not "seal in the juices," or anything of the sort—science has shown us that no such action takes place. (I suspect that this canard derives from the fact that searing often provides a touch of browned, burnt flavor gratifying to the palate.) Stews of this sort include the justly feared British beef stew, as well as the beery Belgian *carbonade Flamande;* the *gibelottes, matelotes,* and *estouffades* of the French provinces; *navarin* of young lamb and baby vegetables, with its sly rustic allusion to infanticide; the spicy, harissa-enlivened *tagines* of North Africa; the warming *broufado* of the Rhône boatmen; the *boeuf à la gardiane* beloved by the Camargue cowboys, after whose job it is named; the homely international clichés of *coq au vin* and *gulyas;* surprisingly easy to prepare Beef Stroganoff, so handy for unexpected visitors; all types of *ragout* and *ragu; stufatino alla Romana; stufato di manzo* from northern Italy; *estofat de bou* from proud Catalonia. I could go on. Notice the difference between the things for which French aristocrats are remembered—the Vicomte de Chateaubriand's cut of fillet, the Marquis de Béchameil's sauce—and the inventions for which Britain remembers its defunct eminences: the cardigan, the wellington, the sandwich.

One authority writes: "Whereas the soul of a *daube* resides in a pervasive unity—the transformation of individual quantities into a single character, a sauté should comprehend an interplay among entities, each jealous of distinctive flavors and textures—but united in harmony by the common veil of sauce." That is magnificently said. One notes that in the United States the now-preferred metaphor to describe the assimilation of immigrants is that of the "salad bowl," supplanting the old idea of the "melting pot," the claim being that the older term is thought to imply a loss of original cultural identity. In other words the melting pot used to be regarded as a sauté, but has come to be seen as a daube.

My choice of pudding is perhaps more controversial than either of the preceding two courses. Queen of Puddings is an appropriately wintry dish, and considerably easier to make than it looks. Mary-Theresa would always serve it after the Irish stew, and it was the first dish I was ever taught to make for myself. Bread crumbs, 5 oz. thereof; 1 tbs. vanilla sugar; the grated rind of a lemon; 2 oz. butter and a pint of hot milk; leave to cool; beat in four egg yolks; pour into a greased shallow dish and bake at gas mark four until the custard is barely set. Gently smear two warmed tablespoonfuls of your favorite jam on top. Are you a strawberry person or a blackcurrant person? No matter. Now whisk four egg whites in a copper bowl until the peaks stand up on their own. Mix in sugar, whisk. Fold in a total of 4 oz. sugar with the distinctive wrist-turning motion of somebody turning the dial of a very big radio. Put this egg-white mixture on top of the jam. Sprinkle a little more sugar on top and bake for a quarter of an hour. One of the disappointing features of this pudding is that it is almost impossible, in writing about or discussing it, to avoid the double genitive "of" which used so to upset Flaubert. But one of the charms of Queen of Puddings (see!) is that it exploits both of the magical transformations the egg can enact. On the one hand, the incorporation of air into the coagulating egg white proteins—the stiffening of egg whites up to eight times their original volume, as exploited in the *soufflé* and its associates. On the other hand, the coagulation of egg yolk proteins—as in custard, mayonnaise, hollandaise, and all variations thereof. Always remember that the classic sauces of French cooking should be approached with respect but without fear.

The first time I made Queen of Puddings was in the cramped, elongated kitchen of our Paris *appartement*. The almost untenable lateral constriction of space in the scullery (which is what it really was) was compensated for, or outwitted by, an ingenious system of folding compartments for storing crockery and utensils. Beyond this room was a small larder from which Mary-Theresa would emerge red-faced, lopsidedly carrying a gas canister, like a milkmaid struggling with a churn. She always insisted on installing a full canister before she began to cook, the legacy of an earlier incident in which she had run out of gas halfway through a stew and had to change canisters in the middle of the process. In the course of doing so she made some technical error, which led to a small explosion that left her temporarily without eyebrows. There was known to be a gremlin in that kitchen who specialized in emptying canisters which by all logic should have been full: the supply had a tendency to run out in the middle of elaborate culinary feats. My father once remarked that all you had to do to run out of gas was merely utter the word "koulibiac."

"It's time for you to learn about cooking," Mary-Theresa said, pressing a metal implement into my palm and holding my hand as we together enacted the motions of whisking, at first using my whole arm and then isolating the relevant movement of the wrist. I experienced for the first time the divinely comforting feeling of wire on copper through an intervening layer of egg, a sound to me which is in its effect the exact opposite (though like most "exact opposites" in some sense generically similar) to the noise of nails on a blackboard, or of polystyrene blocks being rubbed together. (Does anybody know what evolutionary function is served by this peculiarly powerful and well-developed response? Some genetic memory of— what? The sound of a saber-toothed tiger scrabbling up a rockface with unsheathed claws? Woolly mammoths, pawing the frozen earth as they prepare their halitotic and evilly tusked stampede?)

It was my mother, oddly, who was most upset by the revelation of Mary-Theresa's criminality. I say "oddly" because relations between them hadn't been entirely without the usual frictions between employer and employee, added to which were elements of the war (eternal, undeclared, like all the hardest fought wars—those between the gifted and the ordinary, the old and the young, the short and the rest) between the beautiful and the plain, an extra dimension to this conflict being supplied by the fact that Mary-Theresa's looks, slightly lumpy and large-pored, with the ovoid-faced sluggish solemnity of the natural mouth breather, were perfectly calibrated to set off my mother's hyacinthine looks: her eyelashes were as long and delicate as a young man's; her subtle coloration was thrown into relief by the overrobust blossoming of Mary-Theresa's country complexion; and the expressive farouche beauty of her eyes (more than one admirer having blurtingly confessed that until meeting her he hadn't understood the meaning of the term "lynx-eyed") was only emphasized by the exophthalmic naiveté of Mary-Theresa's countenance, which had a look that never failed to be deeply bullyable. Furthermore, there was also a tension of the type—mysterious and uncategorizable but immediately perceptible, as present and as indecipherable as an argument in a foreign language—that occurs between two women who do not "get on." This was apparent in the certain *ad feminam* crispness with which my mother gave Mary-Theresa instructions and issued reprimands, as well as Mary-Theresa's demeanor, with just the faintest bat-squeak of mimed reluctance as she acted on my mother's ukases, her manner managing to impute an almost limitless degree of willfulness, irrationality, and ignorance of basic principles of domestic science on the part of the spoiled chatelaine of the chaise longue (perhaps I paraphrase slightly). All this was underscored by the contrast with Mary-Theresa's attitude to what my mother would call "the boys," meaning my father (never boyish, incidentally, not even in the blazered photographs of his youth, which admittedly record a period before most people felt entirely unselfconscious in front of a camera) and me and my brother: Mary-Theresa's manner with us always having a friendly directness that my mother, with finer perceptive instruments than we possessed, I think saw as not being wholly free of all traces of flirtatiousness. (Has any work of art in any medium ever had a better title than *Women Beware Women*?) All this, of course, would be apparent (or not apparent) in dialogues which, if transcribed, would run, in full, as follows:

MOTHER: Mary-Theresa, would you please change the flower water.
MARY-THERESA: Yes ma'am.

—the live flame of human psychology having flickered through this exchange like the sparrow flitting through the hall in Bede's history. (There is an erotics of dislike.) Anyway, notwithstanding that, my mother reacted badly to what happened. It began one sharp morning in April. My mother was at her mirror.

"Darling, have you seen my earrings?"

Remarks of this nature, usually addressed to my father but sometimes absentmindedly to me or my brother, more as local representatives of our gender than as full paternal surrogates, were a routine occurrence. My father was in the small dressing room next door that opened off their bedroom, engaged in the mysteries of adult male grooming (so much more evolved and sophisticated than the knee-scrubbing, hair-combing, and sock-straightening that my brother and I would quotidianly undertake): shaving (with a bowl and jug full of hot water drawn from the noisy bathroom taps and then thoughtfully carried to his adjoining lair in order to make way for the full drama and complexity of my mother's toilette), eau-de-cologning, tie-tying, hair-patting, cuff-shooting, and collar-brushing.

The earrings in question were two single emeralds, each set off by a band of white gold, in my view possessing the unusual quality of being vulgar through understatement. They were the gift of a mysterious figure from my mother's early life, the love-smitten scion of a Midlands industrial family, who (in the version that emerged through veils of "This weather reminds me of someone I was once very fond of" and "I always wear it today because it was a special day for someone I'd prefer not to speak about") had refused to accept the earrings back when she attempted to return them, and had subsequently run away to join the Foreign Legion. His relatives managed to catch him in time because he was struck down in Paris (in the course of what was supposed to be his last meal as a free man) by a polluted *moule.* In later life he was knighted for services to industry before dying in a Caribbean seaplane crash. The gleaming banks of seafood on display at the great Parisian brasseries are like certain politicians in that they manage to be impressive without necessarily inspiring absolute confidence.

"Which earrings?"

"No, darling, Maman is busy"—this to me—"the emeralds."

"Not in the morning!"

"I wasn't going to wear them, darling—I'm looking in the box."

"Have you tried the box?"

The formulaic, litanic quality of these exchanges is perhaps perceptible in that reply of my father's.

"Of *course* I wouldn't wear them now I'm not an *idiot,*" said my mother.

The discovery of the earrings hidden under Mary-Theresa's mattress in the traditional little attic room of the *bonne* was, to my mother especially, a shock. It was the gendarmes who found the cherished jewelry—the gendarmes whom my father had called, reacting to my mother's insistence at least partly in a spirit of exhausted retaliation, a cross between an attempt to show up my mother's as-he-said hysteria and an *après-moi-le-déluge* desire to give up and let the worst happen (the worst being, in his imagination, I don't know quite what; I think he thought either that the emeralds would turn up somewhere they had been irrefutably left by my mother—beside the toothpaste, down the side of a chair—or that they would have been stolen by the concierge, an especially grim widowed Frenchwoman *du troisième âge,* about whom my father observed that "it's very hard to imagine what Madame Dupont's husband must have been like, once one accepts that circumstances can be shown to rule out Dr. Crippen"). But I think my father had underestimated the French seriousness about property and money. The young gendarme to whom he made the initial report, filling out a form of great complexity, was genuinely and visibly affected by news of the value of the missing items, and turned up at our flat the next day, good-looking and polite, with his *képi* clutched in front of him in a gesture which made him look like a schoolboy apologizing for being late. The policeman, very fair, with the flaxen hair of some Normans, had the air and the manners of being too nobly born for his job— a *vicomte*'s younger son, perhaps, putting in his year or two on the beat (*noblesse oblige* being one of those expressions whose Frenchness is not accidental) before leap-frogging to some glamorously deskbound job in the apparat, tipped for the top. He first sequestered himself in the drawing room with my mother, who ordered tea. And then, before beginning his search, he spoke to my brother and me, first together, with our mother present, and then separately (this arrangement, and my mother's scented departure, smiling and glancing reassuringly and perfect-motherishly backward, being conveyed between the two of them with an apparently wordless complicity that in another context would have seemed tinglingly adulterous). The general overwhelmingness of the occasion was augmented by the feeling that the imputation of theft, once aired, had somehow taken on a life of its own—as if the allegation, when voiced, was, like magnesium, spontaneously combustible when exposed to oxygen. As indeed it turned out to be, though as so often happens with adult dramas that take place in front of children, the first stages were hidden and offstage, perceptible only through the distortions that affected our day. These began when, after potterings and meanderings around the flat on the part of the gendarme—while we sat by the drawing room with Mary-Theresa and our mother, my brother as usual daubing away with an indoor easel and myself reading, I happen to remember, *Le Petit Prince*—he came back into the room and, avoiding all our gazes, asked my mother if he could speak to her alone for a moment.

And now I have to admit to feeling a considerable degree of relief. (There is no more powerful emotion.) These meditations on winter food have been written—and I set down these words with a sense of rabbit-brandishing, curtain-swishing-aside, non-sawn-through-female-assistant-displaying bravura—as the introductory note attested they would be, in midsummer, at the start of my "hols." To disclose the truth in full, I have been dictating these reflections on board a ferry during an averagely rough crossing between Portsmouth and St-Malo, a journey I must admit to having often found frustratingly intermediate in length—neither the hour-long hop to Calais, allowing time merely for a cup of bad coffee, the crossword, and a couple of turns of the deck, nor the day-long full-dress crossing of Newcastle to Göteborg or Harwich to Bremerhaven, which at least offer a gesture in the direction of a proper sea voyage. Portsmouth–St-Malo does, however, have the benefit of depositing one in the most satisfactory, or least unsatisfactory, of the French port towns (an admittedly uncompetitive title, given that Calais is unspeakable, that Boulogne has seen the planners finish what the Allied bombardment began, that Dieppe involves an unthinkable departure from Newhaven, that Roscoff is a fishing village, and that Ostend is in Belgium). With the aid of a seductively miniaturized Japanese dictaphone I have been murmuring excoriations of English cooking while sitting in the self-service canteen amid microwaved bacon and congealing eggs; I have spoken to myself of our old flat in Bayswater while sitting on the deck and admiring the dowagerly carriage of a passing Panamanian supertanker; I have pushed through the jostling crowd in the video arcade while cudgeling myself to remember whether Mary-Theresa used jam or jelly in her Queen of Puddings, before it struck me (as I tripped over a heedlessly strewn rucksack outside the *bureau de change*) that she had indeed used jam but had insisted on its being sieved—a refinement which, as the reader will not have been slow to notice, I have decided to omit. In all memory there is a degree of fallenness; we are all exiles from our own pasts, just as, on looking up from a book, we discover anew our banishment from the bright worlds of imagination and fantasy. A cross-channel ferry, with its overfilled ashtrays and vomiting children, is as good a place as any to reflect on the angel who stands with a flaming sword in front of the gateway to all our yesterdays.

The sea's summer glitter is made tolerable by my newly acquired pair of sunglasses, a proprietary brand of which you have almost certainly heard. Today's breeze is a degree or two cooler than one might in all justice expect it to be, though the chill is kept off by the unfamiliar warmth of my new deerstalker, which I am currently wearing with the earflaps lowered but with the chinstrap untied. I now feel the need to take a stretch around the promenade and inhale deep drafts of sea air through the slight tickle of my false moustache.

Another Winter Menu

Seasons, times of the year, can be strongly evocative of place. Perhaps this is most apparent in spring, which attracts associations with particular periods of youth—especially with the time when an individual feels himself starting to emerge sexually from the bud of childhood, experiencing preconscious urgings and inchoate stirrings which seem to have a parallel in the beckoning mildness of the air and the fructifying, shamelessly suggestive unfoldings and emergings of nature herself. These recrudescences bring with them the memory, the associative baggage, of the original irruption: the landscape on which the *neiges d'antan* once fell. A young woman with whom I recently had the pleasure of conversing admitted that, for her, the onset of spring always brought back the sensation of a particular canalside walk she used to take on her way back from school in the evenings; the incipient summer-hung stillness of the water; the midges; the heat-retaining reeds; the (very) occasional passage of a barge in its bright new livery of spring paint; the bench where she knew she would first be kissed—and this in Derby!

For my own part, the smell of spring air—that smell which is more a texture than an odor, a sense of the atmosphere's near-palpability, and yet a smell as well, the smell of things above the threshold of sensory perception but below the level at which a name may be given to that which is perceived (just as some children, myself once among them, can hear the faint elusive musical tintinnabulation produced by the Brownian motion of air molecules, an ability lost as the bones of the skull and tympanum thicken into adulthood—an irrecoverable, irreparable loss, the loss of something which can never be restored or reduplicated or recovered; as soon as one once cannot hear Brownian motion it is lost, lost for ever, surviving only as the sense of ghost noise, of sounds too delicate and fine to be real, disturbing the perceived with a memory of what can no longer be perceived); similarly the smells of spring duck below the border of nameability and definition. It is the smell of possibility, of imminence and immanence. For myself, this almost sexual sense of renascent possibility transports me back to the south of France, on my first solo visit there at the age of eighteen; it brings with it the smell of wild herbs (with thyme dominant), the silvery underside of wind-stirred olive leaves, the plasticky sheen of new-picked lemons, the texture of a pebbled driveway felt through the rope soles of one's espadrilles; nights spent under a single sheet with the moon huge and proximate. In later, fuller summer, the sense of smell is more acute at either end of the day, before or after the full suppressing heat of the afternoon; the onset of evening brings with it not only the renewal of human movement and busyness and the physical expansiveness and spaciousness that accompany the remission of great heat, but the rebirth of odors which, in some mysterious way, are locked up by the sun to be released by the cooling air of evening—the smell of trees, of settling dust, of water.

Winter brings with it a comparably strong sense of place, transporting me back to our flat off the rue d'Assas. The first serious snowfall of the year would always be the occasion for great excitement: I would demand the attendance of Mary-Theresa and my brother, and the three of us—nanny, older sibling, and thoroughly mufflered and mittened, duffel-jacketed, and balaclaved *protégé,* so protected from the elements that I was practically spherical—would head off into the Luxembourg Gardens to build the first snowman of the year. There would be flurries and eddies of snow as we waddled through the as yet uncleared streets; then, as we reached the gates of the park, Bartholomew would give a yell, drop my hand, and whoopingly construct a snowball which, after first miming a throw of life-endangering velocity, he would lob toward Mary-Theresa, who would gigglingly half-turn away and allow the missile to explode on her shoulder.

"I can fly!" Bartholomew would shout, running through the park with his arms outstretched as he mimed an airplane waggling its wings and banking from side to side. Mary-Theresa and I would hurriedly fabricate our own snowballs and aim them at my transported sibling; my throws childishly underpowered but cunningly timed and precisely aimed; Mary-Theresa's wild, blind, and with that curious double-jointed ungainliness that even beautifully coordinated women manifest when they throw things. Then Bartholomew would tire of his more strenuous cavortings and join us in the construction of a snowman, built on the classic model of big lower blob for stomach and legs, smaller blob for upper body, smallest blob for head, apples for eyes, carrot for nose, laterally wedged-in slice of cake for mouth, discredited saucepan for headgear.

"A fine figure of a man," Mary-Theresa would say, every year, as we stood side by side in front of our handiwork, panting and steaming like racehorses. Then we would trudge back to the flat. A snowstorm that had been in tentative remission when we went out would now have entirely abated, leaving the stars, seen from the unlit park, hallucinatorily bright and clear; when I first heard the biblical expression "breath of life" I instantly saw again the pouring clouds we would exhale on our walks home through the Paris night.

It is against this background that I imagine a winter meal, which should of its nature depend on the piquant juxtaposition of darkness, cold, unhousedness, exclusion (and by implication, fear, disorder, madness) with light, warmth, indoorsness, inclusion (comfort, order, security, sanity). In this sense a winter meal is paradigmatic of the talismanic function of the menu one mentioned in one's preface; and though the act of eating has other ceremonial aspects—celebratory of emotions as divergent in intensity as outright triumph and simple familial well-being—the basic opposition of order and disorder which underlies all structured eating is more keenly apparent in winter, when the hoot of the owl is so easily mistaken for the wail of the banshee, and impossible monsters lurk in the wavering shadows.

Goat's Cheese Salad
Fish Stew
Lemon Tart

It is a common fallacy to assume that winter food should partake of the obvious associations evoked by winter: large viscid stews, unspillably thick soups, colossal puddings. One wants to be warmed, true, but one also wants to be reminded of better times; to feel the onset of dawn in the darkest hour that immediately precedes it. This menu is designed and intended to give a sense of warmth, sunlight, the same feeling of opening out of the year ahead that one gets when encountering one's first glimpse, in January, of the upthrusting tenacious insouciant virginal snowdrop. In this process it is essential to give the necessary attention to the selection of salad leaves. (In themselves the availability of these leaves even in the depths of winter testifies to a kind of modernity and belatedness; our ancestors would have been profoundly disturbed by the thought of January lettuce.) The best procedure is to select your greengrocer with care and then to fling yourself on his mercy. Remember to mix leaves from a variety of different lettuces (Cos, Webb's, romaine, not the appropriately named iceberg, radicchio, chicory).

Make a vinaigrette. My preferred portions are a controversial seven parts olive oil to one part balsamic vinegar; the same proportions as in the ideal dry martini. In what I subsequently came to think of as my aesthetic period, during my early and mid-twenties, I used to serve a seven-to-one martini of Beefeater gin and Noilly Prat vermouth, stirred with large ice cubes and then poured into chilled cocktail glasses; twist of lemon on top, releasing a fine invisible spray of citric juices. As a subsequent refinement I borrowed W. H. Auden's technique of mixing the vermouth and gin at lunchtime (though the great poet himself used vodka) and leaving the mixture in the freezer to attain that wonderful jellified texture of alcohol chilled to below the point at which water freezes. The absence of ice means that the Auden martini is not diluted in any way, and thus truly earns the drink its sobriquet "the silver bullet." In his autobiography, the Spanish film director Luis Buñuel says that the correct way to make a martini is simply to allow the light to pass through the vermouth on the way to striking the gin, in a method analogous to the Immaculate Conception. (He means the Virgin Birth—a common mistake.) I have to admit to never having found that particular vein of intensely Catholic irreligiosity at all amusing.

While it is true that a dry martini should be served unbruised—i.e., still translucent, hence the traditional emphasis so self-consciously defied by James "Shaken Not Stirred" Bond—a vinaigrette should be lightly agitated with a fork until it becomes cloudy and emulsified, the work of a few seconds. It is striking that the Slavic word for the locally distilled spirit, *vodka,* is an affectionate diminutive of the word for water, *voda;* and hence a cognate term to that used in France (*eau de vie*), Scandinavia (*akvavit*), and Ireland (*uisque-baugh,* the water of life). Those oldtimers certainly knew a thing or two.

Arrange the leaves around the sides of the plates on which they are to be served. Luxuriantly nap them with your vinaigrette. Toast a number of slices of bread, one per person, and then put a *tranche* of goat's cheese on each slice and pop them all under the grill. Remove just as the cheese starts to bubble and brown. Place toast and cheese in the middle of the dressed plates and serve. A simple dish but one with pleasant contrasts of heat and coolness, the freshness of the salad and the gamey warmth of its proteinous counterpart.

Cheese is philosophically interesting as a food whose qualities depend on the action of bacteria—it is, as James

Joyce remarked, "the corpse of milk." Dead milk, live bacteria. A similar process of controlled spoilage is apparent in the process of hanging game, where some degree of rotting helps to make the meat tender and flavorsome—even if one no longer entirely subscribes to the nineteenth-century dictum that a hung pheasant is only ready for eating when the first maggot drops onto the larder floor. With meat and game, the bacterial action is a desideratum rather than a necessity, which it is in the case of cheese—a point grasped even in Old Testament times, as Job reveals in his interrogation of the Lord: "Hast thou not poured me out as milk, and curdled me like cheese?" The process of ripening in cheese is a little like the human acquisition of wisdom and maturity: both processes involve a recognition, or incorporation, of the fact that life is an incurable disease with a hundred percent mortality rate—a slow variety of death.

Still, there are a lot of very good cheese shops in France, as I had occasion to remark earlier this very day. (I am dictating these words in the bath of my acceptable little *hôtel* in St-Malo. If one drops a battery powered object into the bath are the results potentially fatal? Memo to myself to check.) I was walking down the rue Ste-Barbe earlier when an unexpected movement a few yards ahead in the street caused me to duck into a small *épicerie* that managed the paradox of being of a higher than usual standard but still typical. The grave-demeanored white-coated *propriétaire,* with a manner that would have been considered reassuringly serious if encountered in an airline pilot or consulting neurosurgeon, was whisking a nine-inch chef's knife over a Carborundum stone, apparently in preparation for tackling the ham that lay silently in front of him on the marble work surface. Four customers, from whom in my flustered state I derived nothing but an impression of shopping-basket–carrying *bourgeois* decorum, turned to register my entrance and then turned away. (One should note that to be *bourgeois* is not at all the same thing as to be middle-class; the former word connotes a precise set of attitudes, prejudices, preconceptions, life options, and political views. Styles of self-satisfaction vary from country to country, just as to be bored is not the same thing as to suffer from *ennui*. The condition of feeling *einsam* is not identical with being lonely, and *gemütlichkeit* is to be distinguished from comfiness.) On my left was a formidable battery of tinned goods, from a definitive brand of asparagus tips to those tinned *petits pois* which have, to more than one palate, intermittently seemed to present a cogent argument for immediate emigration. Behind the counter was arrayed a world-beating selection of hams and prepared pork goods: tasty *jambon à l'américaine,* moreish *jambonneau,* reliable *jambon de York* (how mournfully seldom encountered in York *lui-même*), shoulder of ham, *jambon fumé, jambon de Bayonne, prosciutto crudo di Parma, jambon d'Ardennes,* three types of *jambon de campagne, saucisson à l'ail,* triple-cooked *andouille, saucissons d'Arles, de Lyon,* a rogue *chorizo* or two, a carefully spelled *kaszanka, andouillette* (so importantly different from its near-namesake), subtle *boudin blanc* made to a secret family recipe, hearty *boudin noir,* luxurious *crépinettes, pâté d'oie, pâté de canard, pâté de foie gras* in a hand-labeled tin decorated with what looked like a not especially talented child's drawing of a goose, *terrine de lapin, pâté de tête* looking a little *triste* and leftover, *terrine de gibier,* assorted quiches and galantines, *gâteau de lièvre,* a gallimaufry of other pies and tarts. To the right of the counter, in a chilled cabinet fronted with plastic strips creating the effect of a deliberately unopaque and titillatingly penetrable venetian blind, were the cheeses. No fewer than five different versions of the chief Norman glory, Camembert, an example of the profitable ideas sometimes born during periods of historical ferment, as the cheese was invented due to a cross-fertilization between the ingredients of the Norman regions and the cheese-making techniques of Meaux, as they were exported to Camembert by the young Abbé Gobert, fleeing the Terror in 1792. Also Livarot, Pont-l'Evêque, Neufchâtel, a Brie which to my perhaps hypercritical eye looked a little chalky at the center, and a rich array of small local cheeses that I would have liked to stay and enumerate were it not that the coast now seemed to be clear and it remained only for me to tip my baseball cap complimentarily to the *épicier* and duck back out of his shop, considerably restored after my unpleasant alarm of a few seconds earlier by my contemplation of his wares.

Later that evening in St-Malo I went to eat fish soup. (Perhaps I should say later *this* evening. I'm still in the bath. An adroit maneuver with my prehensile right big toe has just satisfactorily topped up the level of hot water.)

It was the end of a midsummer day; the rich yellow light at the close of the long afternoon came slanting sea-scented across the port like the memory of Cornwall. Perhaps, just as every love stands in some relationship to our first love affair—a relation which holds only if one extends the possible nature of the interdependency to include parody, inversion, quotation, pastiche, operatic recasting, as well as slavish and identical reduplication—no restaurant in later life comes entirely unaccompanied by some associations with our first restaurant. And just as one's first love is not automatically or necessarily one's first bed-partner, and just as well, one's first restaurant is not or need not be one's literal first restaurant, the place where one ate in public for the first time and paid for the experience (the forgotten motorway service station on a trip north to Auntie's, the first, good-behavior–rewarding shopping expedition teashop scone), but rather the place where one first encountered the blinding, consoling hugeness of the restaurant *idea.* Stiff napery; heavy, gravity-laden crockery; pristine wineglasses, erect and presentable as Guardsmen on parade; an expectant commando of pronged, edged, and expectant cutlery; the human furniture of the other diners and the uniformed waiters; above all, the awareness that one has finally arrived at a setting designed primarily to minister to one's needs, a bright palace of rendered attention. Hence, perhaps that tug of the mythic which underlies restaurants, which are after all a comparatively recent institution, evolving out of the traveler's inn, via the gradual urbanization of Western man, and first appearing in their the-atricalized modern lineaments comparatively late, in the last years of the eighteenth century, not long before the Romantic idea of genius (q.v.). There are certain types of conversation, certain varieties of self-awareness, which only take place in restaurants, particularly those bearing on the psychodynamics of relationships between couples, who (frequent solitary diner-out that I am) I notice often eat out apparently with the specific purpose of monitoring the condition of their affair, as if breaking up were something that, by fixed anthropological principle, can only be done by installments and in public; as if it were reassuring to witness how many others were also precariously aboard the freighted craft of couplehood; as if all couples were by law compelled to take their place in a tableau of relationship conditions, with every state on display from the initial flirtatious overextension of eye contact to one of those silences which can only be incubated by at least two decades of attritional intimacy.

Perhaps I was sensitized to all this by my mother. It was with her that I underwent my own restaurant *rite de passage,* and she could be relied upon for very little else as confidently as she could for her sense of occasion. (Of course there had already been other meals eaten out, comparable—to refer back to my previous metaphor—with the rudimentary fumblings and yeti-like gropings of early sexual experience.) The town, Paris; the restaurant, La Coupole; the cast of characters, my mother and me and our Parisian public and an attendant chorus of bustling

45

solicitous waiters; the meal, a fish soup followed by the celebrated *curry d'agneau* for her, a simple *steak-frites* for little me, followed by a lemon tart split between the two of us (and this is something for which I am not going to be bothered to give a recipe: simply purchase the relevant pudding from someone authoritative); my mother's dress, a magnificently expensive black scallop-backed item by a named designer, worn with no jewelry apart from the already mentioned pair of earrings; my own outfit an entirely adorable little blue sailor suit with white neckings. (Many were the hot-eyed glances I had no doubt been unheedingly darted; though one was amused to come across, reproduced in a magazine article, a photograph of the original youth who had so affected Thomas Mann, and upon whom he had modeled Aschenbach's *visione amorosa*—the child in question could only honestly be described as a *lump.* Art over life once again.) It may have been in those moments that food crystallized for me as a lifelong passion, and that a commitment to a particular *modus vivendi* was decided, as she smiled at me across the remains of the tureened soup and devastated *rouille* and said: "One day, *chéri,* I am sure you will do great things."

It will therefore surprise no one to learn that all fish soups and stews have always had an especially high place in my esteem and affections. I have a particularly strong identification with that recipe which fuses the base with the noble, the leftover catch at the bottom of the fisherman's net (the primary source for the fish in this dish as in most fish stews and soups) with the highest degree of esculence, delicacy, and artistry; which brings together the unsalable minnows of the Mediterranean with the fabulous luxuriousness of saffron (almost as expensive, pound for pound, as gold, for which it can sometimes seem to be a kind of edible simile). A dish rooted in the solid traditions of peasant cookery—nicely exemplified by the fact that the dish is prepared in a single pot, the totemic single pot of European and indeed global peasant cookery, from the subsistence farmer in Connemara to the *muzhik* of Omsk—but which also has its noble place in the ramifying, allusive grammar of French restaurant cooking, the cuisine that has in its home country reached the greatest degree of approximation to the full complexity of an articulated language; in short, I have always been especially keen on *bouillabaisse.* As Curnonsky said, "a great dish is the master achievement of countless generations." Bouillabaisse's combination of luxuriousness and practicality, of romance and realism, is positable as characteristic of the Marseillais themselves, who possess in marked degree that habit of seeming to live up to a collective stereotype which is often to be found in the inhabitants of port towns. One thinks of the self-consciously abrasive and warmhearted vitality of Naples, the self-consciously waggish sentimentality of Liverpool, the self-consciously romantic stevedores of Alexandria or even the self-consciously muscular, rude, and truculent dockworkers of old New York. On this spectrum the Marseillais take the place of being self-consciously romantic about how realistic they are, and just

47

as it can seem as if the whole of Liverpool is constantly engaged in the description, celebration, and praise of Scouseness, the Marseillais can appear to be embarked on a permanent project to enumerate, categorize, and enact their own particular brand of forcefully realistic *meridional-ité.* Note that even the name *bouillabaisse* (from *bouillir* and *abaisser,* "boil" and "reduce") strikes a note of swaggering, shrugging, stylized rough practicality, as if to say, it's a soup—what else are you going to do? It is also present in the story underlying the myth that bouillabaisse was invented by the goddess Aphrodite herself, patron saint and founder of that characterful city; a fiction no doubt superimposed upon the historical truth that Marseille was first settled by the Phoenicians, who were attracted by its conveniently near-rectangular natural harbor (whose heart is still the *vieux port*); they brought with them their mythology, their lighthouses, and their talent for trading. Aphrodite is said to have created bouillabaisse as a way of getting her husband Hephaestus—the crippled smith, patron of craftsmen and cuckolds—to ingest a large quantity of saffron, a then famous soporific, and so to fall asleep, thus permitting the goddess to set off for an assignation with her *innamorato* Ares (who has always struck me as being, of all the characters in the Greek pantheon, the most unattractively sweaty). The Greek myths, like the Old Testament, do have the virtue of describing the way people actually behave.

My research has failed to confirm or deny the scientific basis of this folk belief about saffron, which is, by the way, a flower, consisting as it does of the stigmas (the pollen-trapping part) of *Crocus sativus.* It takes more than four thousand of the laboriously (manually) harvested stigmas to provide a single ounce of the spice, the popularity of which is confirmed by the name of the town Saffron Walden, now no doubt a dreary market town with the standard appurtenances of lounging skinheads swigging cider on the steps of the graffiti-defaced war memorial, and a punitive one-way system. I have never bothered to visit Saffron Walden, notwithstanding the fact that it is not a big detour off the route I usually take from my pied-à-terre in Bayswater to the cottage in Norfolk. This part of England, I often think, must have been at its most comfortable during the period of Roman occupation, when toga-clad Romano-Britons could stroll through properly laid out paved streets past clean buildings to the baths, where they could relax with a leisurely dip, a gossip, and perhaps a glass or two of locally grown wine, confident in the knowledge that they were protected from their own countrymen by handsome, polite, heavily armed legionaries. The important thing to remember about saffron from the cook's point of view is that it is enough to use just one or two threads; any more will risk imparting a bitter, "socky" flavor.

There is considerable debate about whether it is possible to make bouillabaisse away from the Mediterranean and the rocky coves that provide this once humble dish with its wondrous variety of what my father used to refer to as "little finny blighters." My own view, which I relate after the consumption of many gloomy so-called bouil-labaisses in northern climes, is that the dish does not travel or translate but that, when the basic principles are understood, it can be made to adapt.

Take two pounds of assorted rockfish, ideally bought somewhere on the Mediterranean in a quayside negotiation with a leathery grandfather and grandson team who have spent the long day hauling nets aboard in steep baking coves, their tangible desire for the day's first *pastis* in no way accelerating the speed or diminishing the complexity of the bargaining process. There must be at least five different kinds of fish, including of course the indispensable *rascasse,* an astonishingly ugly fish whose appearance always reminds me of our Norwegian cook, Mitthaug. Also necessary are gurnard, monkfish/anglerfish/*lotte/baudroie* (the same thing, *baudroie* being the Provençal and *lotte* the French), and a wrasse or two, either the *girelle* or the wonderfully named *vieille coquette,* which I first ate in the company of my mother. Clean the fish and chop the big ones into chunks. Organize two glasses of *provençale* olive oil and a tin of tomatoes; alternatively you can peel, seed, and chop your own tomatoes. Personally, canned tomatoes seem to me to be one of the few unequivocal benefits of modern life. (Dentistry, the compact disc.) In a large, handsome saucepan, sweat two cloves of chopped garlic in one glass of the oil, add the tomatoes and a pinch of saffron; then add six pints of what in England would be chlorinated former effluent (also known as "water") and boil furiously. Put in the firmer textured of the fish and the second glass of oil and boil hard for fifteen minutes. Add the softer textured fish and cook for five minutes. Serve whole fish and big chunks on large soup-plate type plates and serve the broth separately with crouton and *rouille.* I can't be bothered to go into details about the *rouille* since my fingers are starting to go wrinkly in the bath here.

Note that bouillabaisse is one of the only fish dishes to be boiled quickly. This is to compel the emulsification of the oil and water; it is in keeping with the Marseillaise origin of the dish that in it oil is not poured over troubled water but violently forced to amalgamate with it. Notice also that bouillabaisse is a controversial dish, a dish which provokes argument and dissent, canonical and noncanonical versions, focusing on issues such as the aforementioned geographically conditioned possibility of making the dish at all, the desirability or otherwise of adding a glass of white wine to the oil-and-water liaison, the importance or unthinkability of including in the dish fennel or orange peel or thyme or cuttlefish ink or severed horses' heads. (On which my personal verdicts are respectively "yes," "no," "yes," "no," "why not," "yes if you wish to make the *bouillabaisse noire* of Martigues," and "only joking.") Some dishes seem to be charged with a psychic energy, a *mana,* which makes them attract attention, generate interest, stimulate discussion, inspire controversy and debates about authenticity. The same is true of certain artists. Again I am not thinking exclusively of myself.

The conditions and prohibitions with which the making of a successful bouillabaisse is hedged around make it a problematic dish for the home cook, at any rate for the home cook who lives more than an hour or so's drive from the coastline between Toulon and Marseille. My house in the Vaucluse is an hour and forty minutes from Marseille, assuming the good weather which is necessary on the twisting roads of the Lubéron. Other fish soups are less contentious in their composition, a fact that may make them appealing for those who are less beguiled than I am by what Spinoza called "the deep difficulty of excellence." In any case, over the years at my homes in Provence and Norfolk (less often in Bayswater) I have cooked *burrida,* the hearty and accommodating Genoese speciality; *cotriade,* the warming and economical potato-oriented Breton dish (sometimes seasoned simply through the addition of seawater); the soothing *matelote Normande,* of which more very shortly; the exuberant Portuguese fisherman's stew *caldeirada,* enough to make any one of us into Lusophiles, and graced with the additional blessing of reheatability in the form of the excellent fish hash *roupa velha de peixe;* the fiery but somehow light, refreshing, life-affirming fish stews of Thailand, spiked with chili and lemongrass and the glamorous but refreshing exoticism of that suddenly convenient country (only hours away!); the paradoxical red-wine–using *matelote* and *raïto,* the former with its disturbingly phallic and alive seeming eel, the latter with its elusive but comforting taste of cod; the equally coddy Basque *ttoro,* its origin betrayed by its telltale unpronounceability (my brother was fond of speculating whether values were reversed in Basque versions of the game Scrabble, so that players only won a single point for using letters such as *q* and *x*); the crude Greek *kakavia* and the egg-and-lemon enhanced *psarósoupa avgolémono;* the tasty Provençal *soupe de poisson* with its punchy *rouille* and promiscuous willingness to accept whatever is put into it (perhaps the most adaptable and portable of all these national soups); the chowders (from *chaudière,* stewpot, a word which also refers to the kind of domestic gas boiler whose explosion was to kill my parents) of North America, expressive of that continent in their hearty emphatic blandness; the delicate *Bergensk fiskesuppe,* which the unfortunate Mitthaug used to prepare with great displays of energy in his attempts to get the freshest possible, indeed the freshest imaginable, cod and *coley*, rising before dawn to go to Billingsgate and returning with fish which, as my father observed, a competent veterinarian ought to have been able to resuscitate; indeed, our own gray little country is almost the only one that fails to have its own indigenous version of fish soup, even the Scots having their surprisingly edible Cullen Skink.

An example of one of the most cookable dishes, and one that manages to retain a certain glamor, is *bourride,* another preparation deeply charged with memories, in this case of my humble abode in the Vaucluse hinterland village of St-Eustache, hardly more than a shack really, with its five bedrooms and the swimming pool that so added to my popularity with certain of my neighbors. In each bedroom a precarious wicker framework is affixed over the windows, with a mosquito net pinned to it; as an eighteen-year-old paying my first visit to the S of F (my brother then and later having a place near Arles) I used to submit his similar netting to obsessively repeated checks lest any fray or rip should betray the room to the invasion of insect life. Not that I had any banal Lawrentian fears of these creatures (though the vision of one of those huge fluttering obscenely delicate and hairy Provençal moths flying into my open mouth while asleep would cause moments of nocturnal discomfort). Their size— mosquitos the size of flies, flies the size of hornets, and moths the size of pterodactyls—and their talent for vehement frustrated buzzings and crashings meant that the ingress into my room of even one of these behemoths (oops) would guarantee me hours of sleepless padding and stalking with a rolled up copy of *Nice-Matin* or *Le Provençal*.

Right: *bourride*. I was taught to prepare this dish by Etienne, a French youth on an exchange scheme who came to stay with us during summer holidays, and who educated me in how to make a version of the dish with the local fish available near our Norfolk cottage, using the olive oil he thoughtfully brought with him. Buy and prepare a number of thick pieces of white fish equivalent to the number of guests at table; the fish may be John Dory (engagingly known in French as St-Pierre, from the visible residue on either side of the fish's peculiarly friendly looking head—or is that just me?—of the thumbprint of St. Peter the fisherman) or brill or monkfish or indeed almost anything, with the proviso that if it is to qualify as a *bourride sétoise* the stew must be composed of monk-fish exclusively. (A famous village feud occurred after an argument about *bourride sétoise* between fractious in-laws: tempers were raised, insults exchanged, rolling pins brandished, cookbooks consulted, opinions vindicated and hotly rebuffed, and a three-decades-long severing of relations was instituted. Now that's a recipe.) Make stock from fish bones and make an *aïoli* (recipe later, later); add one more egg yolk per person. Chop two leeks and two shallots and sweat them in oil. Add the fish, pour the stock over, and cook until done or just cooked through—about quarter of an hour. Remove the fish, reduce the sauce by an amount that feels appropriate—one third minimum, two thirds maximum. Then pour in the enriched *aïoli*, off the heat, and return whisking to the stove until it achieves the texture of thick cream.

It was on an evening when I had prepared a bourride that I received my first visit from Pierre and Jean-Luc, my Provençal semi-neighbors. They were (are) a pair of brothers of very great antiquity, weathered, skeptical, stupid-intelligent in the classic peasant manner, brusque, full of unpredictable unrefusable kindnesses, and not very tall; and despite both being almost completely blind—opinion in the village varying as to whose eyesight was strictly speaking worse—addicted to shooting. Pierre, the elder of the two, is also the darker, the taller, the more liver-spotted, and much more likely to visit on his own than Jean-Luc; he is also, by a fine margin, the more silent. He never looks directly at one but his avoidance of one's eye somehow manages not to seem either shifty or apologetic; it is as if he were a polite basilisk, courteously failing to avail himself of his ability to turn us all to stone. The three or four partially feral cats who frequent my house during the months I spend at St-Eustache, who always have an air of feline condescension in permitting my co-habitation, are always mysteriously absent during Pierre's visits, perhaps fearing that this Gorgonian power might vent itself on them as they scuttle about on the floor and, in the etymologically radical sense of the term, leave them astonished. On the other hand, perhaps some super-sensory perception informs the cats that if they stray across the paths of the brothers they run the risk of being shot. Jean-Luc, physically distinct from his brother in the ways outlined, is also atmospherically distinct, with an air of mild general affability not at all dispelled by the fact that he is never to be seen without his shotgun, a long, fearsome, single-barreled instrument with marked affinities to a cartoon blunderbuss; he always carries the weapon either broken open over the crook of his arm or—much more alarmingly—resting vertically in the "shoulder arms" position. They live alone together in a little *cabanon* or shepherd's hut about three miles away and are, in fact, relatively rich, owning a great deal of land in the area, including all the area immediately around my own humble property. Their territory is given a wide berth in the hunting season. They are feared and respected eaters. Their visits never fail to precipitate a cryptic exchange on the subject of the weather, of farm prices, an anti-German anecdote or two, a silent and evidently merciless scrutiny of whatever is being prepared for supper that evening, and an often equally cryptic, subtly menacing presentation of gifts: a guinea fowl that has been drowned in homemade *eau de vie,* its little beak held under by Jean-Luc's powerful grimy hands, or a line-caught fish that has been suffocated rather than clubbed to death. On that first visit, though, Pierre and Jean-Luc, dropping in to introduce themselves, caught sight of the bourride I was preparing and, both standing over me as I made finishing touches to the seasoning, pronounced the immortal verdict *"Bon,"* a compliment which got our relationship off to a good start. I was to develop an affection for the brothers that subsequent events did nothing to efface.

From contemplated soups, theoretical soups, hypothetical, remembered, and virtual soups I—though sadly not you, reader, and more's the pity since I think you would have enjoyed it if you had been there—must now return to the real thing. After a splendid coastal evening in St-Malo, I, at the end of a happy afternoon pottering around the reconstructed streets, was in search of that desirable preparation, another standing reproach to our country's depleted culinary culture, the *matelote Normande.* (Why are there not equivalent soups in the British Isles, with Newcastle and Ramsgate vying to outdo each other in the sophistication of their local specialities, and ferocious arguments being conducted over whether samphire can legitimately be included in the eponymous pottage of Cardiff?) It is pleasant, to saunter as if aimless through the streets of a town such as St-Malo, one-eighth sleepily provincial, one-eighth practical and fishermanly workmanlike, and three-quarters tourist-oriented, gift-shopped, and multiply hotelled. The narrow streets, hostile to traffic, give the town the air of hiding from the sea, as if the houses were a form of collective security, a cramped human identity defined in opposition to the life sustaining, death dealing, fish yielding, widow making alien expanses of water. As in so many seaside towns, the architecture and topography are such that the sea itself comes as a surprise glimpsed at the end of a steep alley, or vividly apparent in the gaps between houses, or reluctantly acknowledged as you turn the corner onto a fortified marina or sudden esplanade (its very width another attempt to keep the water at bay), but with its presence betrayed all the time by the smell of ozone and the bad-tempered cawing of hungry gulls.

A stroll through these streets brought me to a little restaurant that—earlier research had already informed me—was mentioned in guidebooks as specializing in *fruits de mer.* The likably straight-faced *patronne* showed me to a flattering corner table, demonstrating, as if it needed to be demonstrated, that always beguiling French attitude of respectful attention toward the solitary diner. The room was narrow and L-shaped, with myself in the far corner of the dog-leg, and it was decorated in a style of acceptably un-ironized kitsch with fishing nets, prints, and wall-hung crustacean pots. Without consulting the menu I ordered a *matelote;* the waiter was impressed.

Scrutiny of one's fellow customers is one of the acknowledged pleasures of dining out. This evening the restaurant was quiet. A group of tourists at the next table was discussing the relative traffic density of different holiday locations, their South German *ich*'s slithery and lubricious; a middle-aged French couple was eating in the traditional Gallic concentrated reverential silence; a widow was dining alone with a small pampered dog across her feet; there was also a young British couple, the man instantly forgettable, of no interest whatsoever, the woman with sun-lightened careless honey-brown hair, hazel eyes that brought the room toward them as if they, and not oneself, were the universe's center of consciousness, something Egyptian about the length and beauty of her neck, wearing a cream-colored dress that shimmered with her movements like windblown wheat, a single band of gold dismayingly visible on one of her long fingers as they absentmindedly curled around a tall wineglass (Entre-Deux-Mers, he had moronically ordered), her bread-breaking movements delicate and heedless, everything about her radiant, enhanced, wasted. This couple had committed the solecism involved in ordering a first course before their now certainly unfinishable *marmite dieppoise*. I caught the eye of the waiter and smiled from behind my "shades."

The discovery among Mary-Theresa's possessions of my mother's earrings (found hidden under the mattress by the polite fair-haired gendarme already mentioned—it was as if Mary-Theresa had been acting out one of the failed impersonations in the legend of the princess and the pea) was a shock, of course, and the scene that ensued was very terrible, not least, one gathered, because of the vehemence and passion with which she categorically asserted her innocence. The news was broken to us children in that way that adult scandals always are—mediated to one's childish self by a sense of things unspoken, by small anomalies in the texture of the everyday, by a feeling of parental distractions and absences, by the knowledge that heated conversations are taking place just out of earshot. So one knew, from the time of one's father's arrival home in the early afternoon—"dropping in on the home front" was what he reported himself as doing—that something was up. At about six o'clock, by which time my brother and I had been alerted by all sorts of major distortions to the daily routine (nonpresentation of tea by Mary-Theresa, my mother instead distractedly constructing sandwiches of, I remember noting, a disturbingly irregular thickness of bread; nonpresence of Mary-Theresa in her putting-the-boys-down-for-their-afternoon-nap role; nonpresence of Mary-Theresa in a supervisory capacity during our afternoon rough-and-tumble; nonpraising by Mary-Theresa of whatever my brother had got up to in the afternoon, her hysterical cry of "Look at what Barry's done now" as she held up his latest daubing or smear being welcomely and conspicuously absent; and finally nonpreparation of tea by Mary-Theresa, what seemed like a slight delay in proceedings gradually extending into a bona fide gastric emergency), my father intervened with his gravely radical tidings.

"Boys, I have some bad news."

The word "boys" inevitably prefaced some announcement of more than usual import—"Boys, your mother is staying for a while in a sort of clinic." In this case:

"Mary-Theresa has been rather naughty, and she has had to leave us."

"But Papa!"

"Please don't ask any more questions, boys. Your mother is very upset and it is important that you show you are strong for her."

Needless to say it did not take too long to piece together the real story, not least because my parents' official declaration of a wall of secrecy had to contend unsuccessfully with my mother's histrionic impulses. She spent the next few days, as she was in certain circumstances prone to do, standing for minutes at a time gazing at the restored earrings in her ears (via a mirror), and was not above muttering, as if to herself, the single word "Betrayed." That evening, uniquely, my father cooked, serving a surprisingly competent sorrel omelette that he must have learned somewhere on his travels, much as he had been taught to juggle by a Neapolitan aristocrat, while waiting in a queue to clear customs during a government employees' work-to-rule in Port Said. Luckily it wasn't one of the times I had part-emptied the gas canister.

· Spring ·

Roast Lamb

A Luncheon on the Theme of Curry

Roast Lamb

Spring, optimum time of the year for suicides, is also an excellent season for the cook. Though I must say that I have often wondered whether, just as Turner invented sunsets, T. S. Eliot may have invented the seasonal surge in the incidence of people attempting to do away with themselves, and whether, before the publication of *The Waste Land,* April was actually, as months go, entirely benign. Notwithstanding that, April, if it didn't used to be the cruelest month, certainly is now—and empirical confirmation of the seasonally adjusted suicide rate was provided by Mary-Theresa's apparently guilt-maddened action in precipitating herself off the Pont-Neuf one crisp

Paschal morning immediately following her exposure. Her body was so heavily weighted with stones (paving stones, stolen or borrowed from a street under repair near the Sainte-Chapelle on the Ile de la Cité) that the policemen who broke the news, two fit young gendarmes, unpuffed themselves by the four-storey walk up to our flat, were impressed by her ability to carry herself as far as the famous bridge with the stones in a bag she subsequently attached to herself, let alone her then managing to heave herself and her burden over the side. Sturdy peasant stock, as my father, not often wrong about people, had observed when initially employing her.

Still, the same factors which make this a difficult time for the manically depressed, the elderly, the memory-tormented, and the weak make it an excellent season for those who are able to congratulate themselves on being in the fortunate position of having survived the winter. And perhaps it is this very element, the resurging triumphant self-delighting competitive rude health of spring, that makes it paradoxically debilitating for those aforementioned types, just as living in beautiful surroundings and in beautiful weather can exaggerate individual misery by giving its victim a feeling of what he is failing to live up to. As a young friend of mine remarked, *à propos* her reluctance to take up a lucrative academic position in Southern California: "Two hundred and fifty days of sunshine a year—what if you still felt miserable?" Perhaps this is only to say that, as the demotic American maxim has it, show me a good loser and I'll show you a loser—and spring is the time when losers are brought face to face with their loserdom, their loserhood. The rest of us rejoice (in the words of the Old Testament), as the sun emerges like a bridegroom from his chamber, rejoicing to run a race.

The appropriate food for this season is combative, uptempo, sanguinary.

Lamb is of course the meat most closely associated, in the Christian tradition, with ideas of violence and sacrifice—in fact, even the most robust of us self-contentedly pagan moderns has been known to experience a slight flicker of distaste at the imagery of the born again being *rinsed in the blood of the lamb.* (One wonders what the mythological force of this image would be if the cleansing agent were, say, baked beans.) And indeed the disturbing literal-mindedness of Christian imagery is seldom as apparent as it is in the practice of eating lamb at Easter. I mean, *really.* This is a particularly off-key custom when one bears in mind the centuries-old association of sheepmeat with the lands where Islam holds its sway. For mutton was originally a staple food of nomadic tribesmen, who favored food cooked in tail fat and loved to spit-roast their charges on their swords. One can imagine Genghis Khan himself, listening to his next day's supper bleating in the field outside his yurt as he stood under the huge star-filled amphitheater of the Central Asian plains, and for the first time began to feel the weight of years. . . . The association of sheepmeat with Islam grew through the development of the cuisines of the Middle East, which include dishes such as the superbly tender and esculent *inmos,* in which mutton is stewed with yogurt and cumin in what must surely be a deliberate inversion of the Hebraic injunction against seething a kid in its mother's milk, through to Islamized and re-Christianized Spain, where an excessive affection for lamb (with its religio-racial associations) could be enough to earn the unfortunate gourmand the attentions of the Inquisition, through to contemporary Britain, where the time-honored religio-culinary coupling is celebrated anew in the exciting proliferation of large-windowed and conveniently situated kebab outlets, there being a number of remarkable examples near my Bayswater pied-à-terre.

The upsurge in animal spirits that accompanies the onset of spring is, of course, partly just that—an exultant *intifada* of our animal nature, the winter-slimmed beast slipping through the bars of its seasonal cage. Many of the ideas about rising sap, quickening pulses and so on, are no more than literally true: I myself, at this time of year when the first scent of the resurrecting flora enlivening my nostrils, used to feel as if I were growing an inch or two taller; my father would take out a mortifyingly dilapidated gray woolen two-piece outfit, a fossil ancestor of the modern tracksuit, and go for his wobbly first bicycle ride of the year; my mother's hats would, as if in response to a chemical reaction, mysteriously change color; my brother, in his mountebankish way, would claim to be felled in his tracks by a seasonal migraine (generally robust, indeed culpably overrobust, in his constitution, he permitted himself this annual bout of malaise). And there was also the strange overexcitement which used to come upon Mitthaug. He was a "recovering" alcoholic, a fact I gradually pieced together, as one does in childhood, from silences, elisions, absences, and that elusive sense of something not being quite right, which children are so quick to intuit, and which provides one reason why they are so alarming to us grown-ups. His normally ebullient mood would go through a marked seasonal dip in or around mid-December. Perhaps, for him, the first snow of the year was too tangible evidence of the imminent full onset of winter: the claustrophobic melancholy of the narrowing year. (The Scandinavian winter, the almost physical sense of constriction it imposes on the psyche, must be a factor in the typical Scandinavian manner of depressive, lugubrious, hibernatory drinking.) But when spring came Mitthaug would dramatically perk up and would reassume his habitual near-manic good humor. His problematic teetotalism, with its paradoxical high spirits, was a sort of backlash against the way he might have been if he was drunk; since, to any really committed career drinker, drunkenness is normality and undrunkenness is exceptional, his sobriety was a way of being, in that all too accurate phrase, "out of his head."

It is inevitable that spring, by providing a visible metaphor for the processes of rebirth, growth, birth, and resurrection, should have become associated with other kinds of nascence and opening-out; this is especially, doubly true in the case of the artist, intimate as he is with sensations of imminent unfolding and budding, of tentative realization swelling into ecstatic apprehension of not-quite-certainty with the rampant unexpectedness of one of those ingenious little packets which, when dropped into water, so startlingly and magically transform themselves into fully inflated, accessorized, and provisioned life rafts.

It was at this time of year, one day after a garlicky haricot-accompanied classic gigot, prepared by my own fair hand in Norfolk at the cottage which is still my primary place of dwelling, that the artistic project which was to form my lifetime's work began its first tentative glimmerings in my imagination—the light it emitted being faint, elusive, detectable only by the most sensitive and finely tuned of instruments, perceivable only by the most dark-adapted of imaginable eyes, like the light cast in a deep cave not by lanterns, torches, or candles, but by the faery luminescence of decomposing moss.

"I was walking in the garden after lunch," I recently recollected for the benefit of an interviewer as we both unspokenly relished the exquisite consonance of torpidly slaloming between ovoid plant beds in the very same garden. "The willow's ringlets were turning green. There was a slight breeze. It suddenly occurred to me that the garden stood as an image for an art designed not to seem like art."

"I'm not sure I follow you," said my delightful interlocutor faux-naively and cunning-little-minxishly, already providing an early instance of the ability to lead one on and draw out one's train of thought so essential in an amanuensis or Boswell—not that she herself in any other

way (least of all physically) resembled that portly opportunistic Caledonian journalizer. As she spoke she leaned
forward and looked up sidelong at me through a fine cur-
tain of wind-mussed palish hair that intensified the eroti-
cizing force of her glance in the same way that the
movement of a light summer dress enhances, by fluidly
half-revealing and half-concealing, the shapeliness and
animal lambency of the female leg. Her eyes were hazel
(everybody's eyes are hazel) but with green radial tiger-
stripe highlights.

"My thoughts had been running on the connection
between gardening and more general patterns of aesthetic
ideology," I said in my twinkly-donnish-but-with-an-
edge-of-sexual-danger way. "The idea of the garden is to
create an image of nature through the highest possible
level of art, while at the same time only permitting a par-
tial awareness of the presence of that art. Similarly, the
rock garden in the Zen temple at Kyoto gains its effect by
the intensity of its absences—it is itself by virtue of what
it is not. It's not so much that 'less is more'—if you will
forgive my ironic waggling fingers—but that less *is* more,
a maximalization of omission."

The whiteness of flowers, the purity of the beloved, the
immanent spring.

"I'm not quite sure what this has to do with anything,"
said my feisty empiricist. We were by now stationary; I
propelled her into movement by holding my arm a half-
inch away from her elbow and moving my eyebrows in
the direction of the geranium beds.

"Ah, but what has anything to do with anything?" I said in my best Continental-imposter mode. "That baking afternoon was when I first started to think seriously about the aesthetics of absence, of omission. Modernism instilled in the responsible creator the sense that certain artistic choices were no longer possible. To write like *X*, to paint like *Y*, to compose like *Z*, became evidence of a failure of seriousness, an unwillingness seriously to inhabit the artistic present.

"From this one moves easily to the realization that an artist's seriousness, the measure of his talent and gauge of his achievement—the triangulatory calculation which permits one to assess the height of his particular massif—is what seems to him to be impossible, undoable, unavailable, forbidden, barred, banned, denied. An artist should be assessed by what he doesn't do: a painter by his abandoned and unattempted canvases, a composer by the extent and intensity of his silence, a writer by his refusal to publish or indeed to inscribe. One quickly comes to realize that *the most important part of any artist's oeuvre is the work he knows it is no longer possible to attempt.* For the artists who charge blindly up these benighted avenues of ordinariness, mediocrity, and publication, one has only the fastidious pitying half-contempt of a great chef escaping a revolution in disguise, traveling in mufti, and forced to stay at a village inn where he witnesses the hostess's destruction of her produce through overcooking and uninstructed technique, the beef charred, the soup watery-lumpy, the vegetables flaccid, the hygiene rudimentary; but he is unable to reveal his knowledge lest it disclose his identity and lead to his death, just as the ignorance of the Marquis de Chamfort, fleeing the French Revolution, caused him to be captured and guillotined when he blurted out that he thought it took a dozen eggs to make an omelette. Thus, the works an artist has in the *fullest* sense created—the works he has most thoroughly thought through and understood—are the works he does not attempt. The artist lives with an idea, inhabits it, probes it, tests it, until he comes to the reason why it is impossible—and then, surely, he has understood it more fully, he has in the strongest sense *created* it more fully, than his less intelligent doppelgänger who fatally and carelessly makes the naive, of course charming, but still moronic error of actually committing his thoughts to paper or canvas or the pianoforte."

"Yeah," said my delightful inquisitor, with an attempt at casual indifference or uninterest that to the tutored eye only revealed all the more starkly her rising excitement, "but how can you tell? I mean, how does anyone know about the books you aren't writing, the sculptures you aren't making, whatever? What's so different from just sitting there on your bum?"

I took the question to be certain proof that our thoughts were running along identical lines.

"The secret princes of thought," I murmured, "who go among us in mufti. But who knows who, who knows whither, who knows whence? Your observation is stirringly trenchant. Genius is close to imposture; the correlation between interestingness and fraudulence is 'disturbingly' high. But perhaps there is some profit in blurring these distinctions, as there is profit in blurring the distinction between art and life."

At the bottom of the garden is a marble seat, bracingly chilly, facing an expanse of water slightly too small to be a flighting pond, but bigger than the goldfish-infested lily pool of the conventional cottage garden. Sedge grasses create an impression of wildness. Reeds and rushes swayed in pharaonic salutation as we arranged ourselves on the cool stone.

"Consider a recent item in the newspapers. A married couple who specialized in that almost oxymoronic discipline 'performance art' had embarked on a new 'work.' They were to start out at opposite ends of the Great Wall of China and walk towards each other with the intention of meeting in the middle. The 'work' was to be 'about' ideas of separation, of difficulty, of distance, the existence of categorical distinctions between the artwork and the life project; about the bankruptcy of traditional forms of self-expression. Little (or indeed big) adventures that took place en route—dietary upsets, route finding mishaps during absent sections of the wall, hilarious misunderstandings and incomprehensions on the part of the Chinese and the walkers—were all to be part of the 'work.'

"That was the intention. But the upshot was otherwise, and has been widely regarded as turning the whole exercise into a fiasco. The male half of the couple, a Dutchman, seems to have undergone a *coup de foudre* and fallen in love with a young Chinese woman in a village he was passing through. Their eyes meeting over the communal rice bowl, that sort of thing. In a flash he realized that his destiny was with this woman and he abandoned his 'other half,' abandoned the 'performance,' and moved into the village until such time as the authorities would give him permission to marry the girl. His unlucky previous inamorata also abandoned the project and flew home to her native Heidelberg and set to the important business of giving denunciatory interviews about her onetime partner.

"Now, this event, this 'disaster,' seems to me to be as moving and poignant an artwork as has been created in the second half of the century—because, after all, who is to say that the work is over? The apparent abandonment, the *coup de foudre,* the disintegration of the original project—these are all surely part of a larger, revitalized project, an artwork which, while treating themes such as inconstancy, chance, infatuation, the romance of the East, and so on, also *genuinely* dissolves the boundaries between art and life, while *radically* challenging the boundarizing and conceptual structure of the old aesthetics. The initial idea for the Great Wall walk had a banal heroism, an outdated rhetorical kookiness. But the refashioned work has genuine transgressive sweep, pathos, surprise, reach, chiaroscuro, as well as a very contemporary acknowledgment of the sheer power of contingency.

"But this is of course to bring us back to the problem you so cogently and movingly raised a moment or two ago, to wit: How is anyone to know? For if the unwriting writer, the unpainting painter, the silent composer, is the greater figure by virtue of not being diminished into actuality, the fact remains that his life's work runs the risk of going unacknowledged, unrecognized, by virtue of going undisclosed. So what to do? As you know, the idea of genius was invented by Giorgio Vasari, a gossipy, intelligent man of surprisingly and surpassingly accurate judgment; Vasari took as his exemplar the figure of the genius Michelangelo—and who can blame him? But amidst the tales of the adversarial relationship between the genius and his milieu (the intractability of his material, the difficulty of his own nature, the obtuseness of patrons) is one radiantly suggestive moment. Piero de' Medici, son of the more famous Lorenzo, following a particularly heavy snowfall in Firenze, a city whose climate is more mutable than one might sometimes suspect, invites the great artist to his palace to make a snowman. We are told nothing more than that this creation was 'very beautiful'—but who can doubt its overwhelming transcendent excellence, its status as what another writer has called 'the finest snowman on record'? Perhaps this, the least permanent, most fugitively evanescent of Buonarroti's works, is the one that speaks most lastingly to our own transience and temporality, our own incarceration within the passing moment—in short, perhaps this snowman can securely (albeit provocatively) be regarded as *Michelangelo's greatest work*.

"And how do we know about this masterpiece? Answer: We would know nothing of this chef d'oeuvre were it not for the testimony of Vasari. The biographer, the anecdotalist, here features as a collaborator, an essential (*the* essential) component in the transmission of the artwork to posterity, to its audience. Here, indeed, is an answer to your question: How do we know? We know because we are told; because there is a witness—'and I alone survived to tell thee'; because the artist's project, the artist's commitment to leaving his own silence unbroken, is not compromised while at the same time being fully conveyed. In other words, the artwork exists because of the witness, and the quality of the witness is the determining factor in the highest order of art, the work of art which exists perfectly, ideally, flawlessly—that's to say, the work which exists only in the minds of the artist and his collaborator the witness. It was in realizing this that I saw that my own artwork, the artwork the outlines of which first came to me in this garden—the artwork which consists of its own intention—needed a collaborator, an apostle, a witness. And it is this partner, companion, evangelist that I have been looking for ever since and who I think we both, all games and pretended indifference momentarily discarded, are beginning to suspect that I might now have finally found."

It was a moment of large solemnity. The great episodes in one's life are often accompanied by a sense of emotion in abeyance, by a pressure of *expected* emotion—the feeling that our schooling has trained us to view as the standard, the received experience. But the falsity of these emotions (triumph and disaster, twin imposters in the fullest meaning of the term; love; grief; or, to take one particular example, gratitude. It has not, I think, been sufficiently stressed that gratitude does not exist: the term has come into being to describe an emotion of which ethics teaches us to demand the existence, for the purposes of moral algebra, of making the equations balance, just as astronomers calculate the existence of invisible stellar masses—the now too much referred-to "black holes"—through their interaction with other, visible matter. But in this case the black hole is genuinely an absence rather than a presence-in-absence, because in the space where "gratitude" is routinely described as existing, there is instead a compound of duty, guilt, and most especially resentment; no action anywhere in the history of the world has ever been undertaken out of gratitude); as I was saying, the fact that these emotions are false manifests itself in our consciousness as the knowledge of an inner lack, an awareness of what we are not feeling. But at the same time we are conscious that something ought to be there—we are aware of the form of the emotion, the structural space it ought to occupy, but not of the content, of the feeling itself. This discrepancy or gap manifests itself as a pressure of expectation, so that most of the great moments of life are accompanied by a subtle sense of anesthetized anticlimax. On this occasion, however, the union of two minds was very great: the emotion was so overbearing that my companion displayed its effects in one of the most vivid and moving ways a human being well can, through an access of "church giggles."

It was while she was suffering this paroxysm, an eruption which testified to the fullness of her submission to the moment, that she uttered the formula that bound her irrevocably to our joint project. In an older, gentler, more confident age one might have said that the sacred oath emerged from the fair grotto of her lips like a priestess descending temple steps; but I will say instead, and simply, that she promised. The last of the giggles, shaking her body like the final hiccuping tremors of an earthquake, were still upon her, giving her tone a levity like that which possessed the holy dancers of the dervish, a Buddhist gaiety and merriment in the midst of the utmost gravity and solemnity, a *sprezzatura,* as she spoke the vow: "My word!"

Not that all lamb recipes are necessarily sanguinary. (Just as well, given the fastidiousness which prevents some people from eating meat on which any trace of blood is visible. My neighbor in St-Eustache, who used to drop in to use the pool with a frequency that betrayed an enviable lack of embarrassment, before she met such a tragic fate, used to ask for meat "well cooked," so that its juices had entirely disappeared. "Why eat it at all, if you're going to eat it like that?" as I overheard one Frenchman remarking to another who had asked for something *bien cuit.*) Poor Mary-Theresa's Irish stew certainly wasn't bloody, and other dishes that involve long, slow cooking of the adaptable beast fall into the same category. Northumbrian duck, for instance, the Northern recipe for lamb shoulder boned and stuffed to impersonate the eponymous water-bird: a dish which displays, within the general context of our impeccably stolid national cuisine, a vein of lurid fantastical imaginative bad cooking comparable to an otherwise impeccably sober-suited Establishment figure (a bishop, say) momentarily hitching up his trousers to betray an alarming glimpse of lime-green socks; other comparable dishes are *djuredi,* which remains one of the few distinctive glories of what used to be the Yugoslav kitchen; the hearty Welsh *cwl;* the odiferous *arni ladorigani* of Greece, pungent with oregano, that misunderstood herb, so indispensable to the manufacture of a successful pizza; the Bulgarian *kapama* in its two versions, one suitable for cooking in spring (onions and garlic), the other in autumn (mushrooms); the undainty Rumanian *tokana.* It is striking to notice how many of these dishes come from countries whose cuisine can be seen as just the *teensiest* little bit primitive. And there is also the Islamic tradition of meat cookery, represented in the United Kingdom by the aforementioned kebab shops and the gratifyingly confrontational window displays of halal butchers, as well as by dishes such as lamb *inmos,* lamb *tagine,* and those masterpieces of the Persian kitchen exhibiting such a fascinatingly intelligent use of apricots.

Indeed, boned shoulder of lamb stuffed with apricots is one of those dishes that effects a revolution equivalent to the Copernican or Einsteinian revolutions, or to one of those discoveries in mathematics (Penrose tiling, Mandelbrot's fractals) which raises the issue of whether the mind in question has discovered the existence of an object pre-existent in some ideal or potential order, or whether the mind has simply *invented* the principle, as one might invent a new kind of screwdriver or frying pan. That is to say, the recipe in question shows that lamb and apricots are one of those combinations which exist together in a relation that is not just complementary, but seems to partake of a higher order of inevitability—a taste that exists in the mind of God. These combinations have the quality of a logical discovery: bacon and eggs, rice and soy sauce, Sauternes and *foie gras,* white truffles and pasta, *steak-frites*, strawberries and cream, lamb and garlic, Armagnac and prunes, port and Stilton, fish soup and *rouille,* chicken and wild mushrooms; to the committed explorer of the senses, the first experience of any of them will have an impact comparable to an astronomer's discovery of a new planet. Perhaps the closest analogy is with the arts: in the course of a lifetime's engagement with any one of them one goes through periods of boredom, ennui, anomie, déjà vu, it's-all-been-doneness; but then, just as exhaustion and fatigue are beginning to set in, just as one grows certain that full familiarity with all possible excitements has been attained, one comes across a new voice or manner or technique whose effect is as revivifying as the discovery of a despaired-of cache of supplies by an Arctic explorer. Thus the intrepid polar adventurer is spared from having to settle down and feast on his own huskies; similarly the discovery of a new artist is a discovery of new resources; viz. one's first encounter with Mallarmé or late Beethoven.

(Stupid people have sometimes even claimed to find something of the sort in my brother's work.)

Complementarity is a deep mystery about taste just as it is about people. There is a profound unity in plurality that comes into being when one meets a spirit that vibrates to the same frequency as one's own; never forgetting that resonance on a particular note is a powerful force of nature—one thinks of the organ note that can demolish a cathedral, or the destructively precise wind velocity that tears down suspension bridges. The contrary principle of dislike, of disaffinity, is of course equally (more?) powerful. For some time after I poisoned Hercule, the hamster Bartholomew was supposed to be looking after, I kept the half-empty packet of rat poison in my little leather satchel and would take it out to look at as one might inspect a photograph of a particularly cherished cousin. The man who sold me the poison, paid for by assiduously hoarded pocket money (I would work out how many sweets I wanted and then halve the amount I permitted myself to buy), himself seemed like one of the exhibits in an especially out-of-the-way and underused pet shop—with his threadbare eyebrows and red-rimmed nostrils he could have been a hamster experiencing the first symptoms of poisoning, or a tortoise only partially emerged from hibernation. As he produced the blue box containing the crumbly bland white powder his demeanor was so undertakerly (my memory recalls a glimpse of shirt-cuff rigid with starch and an imperfectly laundered white coat) that, at the moment the packet and my thriftily preserved francs changed hands, a gremlin of insouciance compelled me to whisper: *"Pour empoisonner le hamster de mon frère."* He smiled—and whether that smile indicated no more than an old-codgerish amusement at what he took to be a schoolboy's flight of fantasy, or a fuller understanding and complicity, I am to this day unsure. When I crumbled the powder into little Hercule's birdseed I was mercifully unaware that a day would come when my fellow human beings would regard such pet food as a comestible fit for themselves. Though I have to admit that there is an acceptable Persian recipe for sunflower seed cake.

The lamb dish whose recipe I choose to give here is the most traditional and straightforward, and also the most excellent, of the French treatments of *gigot d'agneau:* it is the Breton recipe for salt marsh lamb, *agneau pré-salé.* (The first time I heard this term I thought that *pré-salé* meant "pre-salted," and referred to the fact that this particular lamb, by virtue of grazing on salt marshes, specifically those around Mont-St-Michel in Normandy, had undergone a kind of internal salting, a preliminary seasoning by the hand of beneficent nature. This is slightly less ridiculous than it might seem when one bears in mind the belief, tenaciously clung to in my own beloved Provence, that the local lamb can taste of the wild sun-dried herbs of the *garrigue,* upon which it diurnally snacks. But I took the term "pre-salted" to be a quintessentially French piece of unsentimental directness in relation to matters gastronomic—as if a carload of children might look out of the window and exclaim: "Look, *maman,* ready-salted lamb!"

The beguiling similarity of *pre* and *pré* is a classic example of the false friend, or *faux ami,* with which English and French are liberally besprinkled. The grammatical congruence between the two languages invites or multiplies the points at which sentences match up side by side, aligning themselves together like cogs, while at the same time proliferating riotously the number of words that do not mean what they appear to mean. To such an extent is this the case, in fact, that the two languages as a whole might be compared to *faux ami.* A suggestive idea. The concept of the false friend of course has a more general applicability and usefulness than in the purely grammatical sphere. Not least in family life.)

Preheat the oven, brush the lamb, six pounds for eight people, with butter and oil, cook for however long it takes. Use a meat thermometer if you have Doubts. A variation is to make incisions with a small knife and then to stud the lamb with slices of garlic and rosemary. The classic Breton accompaniment to lamb is a dish of flageolet beans.

The attentive reader will have noticed that I have not given a menu suggestion to accompany this dish. It is time to do so.

Omelette
Roast Lamb with Beans
Peaches in Red Wine

This custom of preceding the meat with an omelette is of course that practiced at La Mère Poulard, the tourist-trap restaurant on Mont-St-Michel, whither, I must confess, my steps sometimes wend on my visits to the northern coast of France. As they did not on this occasion. There is something about the most visited of the world's beauty sites and "interesting" places that gives a quality of banality to the most astonishing scenes. The temple friezes at Mahabalipuram, the skyscrapers of New York, have that already-seen texture of experiences rendered familiar in advance by television and guidebook. Mont-St-Michel is, obviously, in the same category, and the crocodile files of tourists streaming up its narrow lanes do nothing to restore the extraordinariness to this extraordinary place— a quality which, like much natural or artistic beauty in the aforementioned genre of the familiar/famous, can only be sensed in the first few seconds of our encounter with it, before the filter of routine descends like a clanging shutter, and one feels that one is listlessly turning the pages of a magazine article, rather than standing rapt before a wonder of the world. My mother, on my first visit to Mont-St-Michel, in the course of an expedition from Paris, stopped the car at the far end of the much-flooded *chaussée* and allowed me to drink in the somehow intensely Celtic sight of the rock in silence. Anxious maidens peering over mist-shrouded battlements, dogs contentedly slumbering under the scarred banqueting table. Although it is, as a rule, easier to give than to receive (and a talent for receiving gifts is far, far more rare than a talent for giving them—one concedes so much more, in the act of reception, whereas to be in the position of the giver is to retain all the psychic appurtenances of power, patronage, and control), this does not apply to moments in time. To be able to give someone a moment of silence, a sight, or a vision, requires an uncommon degree of psychic tact, and one can imagine the sense of violation and disquiet introduced into this perfect instance of silent communion when my brother interrupted the still rhapsody with an explosive belch and a gruff demand as to the timing of lunch, followed by a leering query as to how often people were caught on the causeway and drowned.

Lunch that day in La Mère Poulard was my first meal eaten in a restaurant recommended by a Michelin star. The theatricality of the omelette-beating made a great impact, and the lightness and delicacy of those omelettes also convinced me of the efficacy of the old wives' tale concerning copper pans. I remember accomplishing from memory a charming little sketch of this scene, which I demurely gave my mother later that same evening; she had just finished calming down the hotel management, following an incident in which my brother had blocked the lavatory with two (!) torn-up copies of *Le Figaro*. He had been conducting primitive experiments in the manufacture of papier-mâché.

The recipe for Mère Poulard's omelette is given in *French Provincial Cooking* by the incomparable Elizabeth David. A Parisian gourmand had written to her to ask the secret of her celebrated dish. Her reply: "*Voici la recette de l'omelette: je casse de bons oeufs dans une terrine, je les bats bien, je mets un bon morçeau de beurre dans la poêle, j'y jette les oeufs et je remue constamment. Je suis heureuse, monsieur, si cette recette vous fait plaisir.*" Notice the dismissive overpoliteness of the valediction: French is particularly well adapted to these insincere grace notes, as the evidence of such phrases as "*je vous prie d'accepter, cher monsieur, l'expression de mes sentiments les plus distingués,*" and so on, convincingly attests. What these pleasantries often mean is well summarized by an expression of one of Bartholomew's wives: "Go boil your head."

My own recipe for omelettes is less of a recipe than it is a set of observations. First, the importance of the pan itself is difficult to exaggerate. One must use a cast-iron pan with a seven-inch diameter and a thick base. This is wiped but never washed. Think of it as a member of the family. Second, the eggs should be given a few turns with a pair of forks and not strenuously and authentically beaten, *pace* Mme Poulard. Third, the butter must be of good quality. Add the eggs when the foam subsides but before it has changed color.

As I have already remarked, however, this trip to France was not to encompass a visit to Mme Poulard's hotel-restaurant. The morning after my fish soup I descended to breakfast in the attractively quiet and out of the way little hotel I had discovered the day before. My fellow customers sat silently over their breakfasts as the angled sunlight poured into the mullioned room. Two ambassadors for *le troisième âge,* the man's expressive silver head clipped and military, the woman's trace of *arrivisme* betrayed by a single strand of pearls (never before luncheon!), greeting one's raffishly belated arrival with an inclination of the head and a mumbled *m'sieur;* a solitary American frowning over the stock market page of the *Herald-Tribune;* a couple of lesbian I-would-imagine schoolteachers, sensibly trousered, multiple-guidebook–consulting; and a family of Britons, the parents struggling to regulate their fractious and oikish progeny, who provided further evidence for a now familiar reversal: whereas in previous generations it was the children who improved on the social standing of their parents, albeit sometimes with difficult human consequences, now the opposite procedure has come into being, and one is often confronted with the shocking but not surprising sight (and how many things in modern life are precisely that combination of shocking but not surprising) of pleasantly spoken, unmistakably middle-class parents, cultured in their interests and aspirations, raising offspring whose accents, attitudes, and pursuits are unabashedly proletarian. There was also a pair of priests, staying at a hotel one would have thought a little too expensive for them; the elder of the two had an eerie long thin El Greco face under a cap of graying brown hair, cut in a pudding-basin shape by plainly amateur hands. The honeymoon couple had not yet come down to break their fast.

Driving a right-hand-drive car on right-sided French roads can be alarming: the farm vehicles, somehow both more rackety and less fundamentally comic than in England, being a particular test of one's neck-craning, the steadiness of one's nerve, the torque exerted by one's engine, and, when driving on country roads, one's ability to judge the left-sided clearance while flashing unfamiliarly close to some stoic muleteer. The transposition of left-to-right is easier to manage if one's mode of transport has been equivalently transposed. I never fail, on experiencing the first few wonderlandish moments after arrival in France, during which the air, the light, the very texture of existence seem to have been subtly altered, enhanced, the possibilities for intelligence and pleasure increased, the switch in the side of the road being an aspect or token of this more general alteration; in those first seconds when one has consciously to force oneself into the mental discipline of looking in the right direction with the cultivated reflex of a man trying to inculcate a habit, as one might practice elocution or a more upright posture, I never fail to think of poor Mitthaug, lurching in front of his onrushing train. For this and other reasons I spent the morning hiring a car, or rather collecting a car hired over the telephone a few days previously—though as anyone who has experience of French procedural overelaboration will know, any such action will always carry a risk of failure through one's lack of foresight in failing to bring one's maternal great-grandfather's birth certificate, or five different proofs of address. No such calamity befell this transaction. The blazered hire-company functionary had a brisk, up-tempo American efficiency that had perhaps been adopted in the same spirit of trans-Atlantic emulation as his impertinent indoor sunglasses. I picked out a combative little Renault 5, sunroofed, manual, nippy rather than powerful, adequate to the task in hand.

I had cunningly forborne to vacate my room before collecting my new car and so now wove back through the narrow *Malouine* streets, making only one navigational error (which deposited me in a slick-washed cobbled courtyard, a residential square as thoroughly shuttered against the morning light as if its inhabitants had been in mourning or in purdah). The action of settling a bill in France, or undertaking any other financial transaction, can have any one of a range of tonalities—brisk, abrupt, openly voracious, oddly intimate, confiding, dismissive—but it is almost always characterized by a certain Gallic intentness. (An aspect of this is that, notwithstanding the noted avariciousness of the French, I have never encountered, read of, or heard about any restaurant bill being in any way padded or doctored, while kitchen shortcuts and fiddles are naturally rife—a deep unintended compliment to the sheer seriousness of money.) In this case, I settled *l'addition* with *Madame la propriétaire* herself. She displayed a good-natured version of that never failing Gallic *interestedness* in money; this took the form of a benign acceptance of what was her due, laced with the faintest imaginable trace of leering acquiescence—her general demeanor that of a brothel madam exchanging formal courtesies with a valued customer, but at the same time unable entirely to suppress her knowledge of his special tastes.

I hefted my suitcase, slammed doors, settled down in the car with a sheaf of maps on the passenger seat and observed the entrance to the hotel from across the street, via the wing mirror. The likely course of the day's drive would be to go along the coast westward into Brittany rather than eastward and north into Normandy proper. (One should note in passing that the Norman diet of cream and apples is still stirringly reminiscent of the hard winters and brutally extensive darkness that must have driven the original Norsemen to seek warmer and less predictable climates.) Mont-St-Michel and the faded glories of the Norman resort coast, so likably overpraised by Proust, were not this time for me. First, though, we would be passing through Dinan, a resort town of the sort that in England would be shabby-genteel and raffish, but which in a French context has the quality of a rational (and maturely tentative) debauchment. Typical that the French should have developed the notion of gambling via the casino (a word which in Italian originally denoted a brothel), applying their talent for categories and schema to the idea of randomness; making a science out of chance, a taxonomy of probability whose basis lies in the human emotions of elation and despair. And making a bit of money in the process, naturally. I shifted in my seat, my sunglasses stylishly warding off the morning glare. Across the street a kerchiefed matron battled her way back from the market.

Our meal, which has so far consisted of an omelette and a roast *gigot d'agneau,* has been a trifle on the heavy side. (Isn't "trifle" a very inappropriate word for trifle?) An appropriate dessert would be refreshing, fresh, light, sharp, clear, bringing a note of Poussinian order, grace, and decorum to the slightly Michelangelesque *terribilità* of the preceding two courses. My personal suggestion would be peaches in red wine, a dish which possesses that very simplicity and directness which can become a kind of more highly evolved complexity—just as one of the most exquisitely sophisticated fashion statements possible is the ultimate, the unsurpassable simplicity of the little black dress, or LBD, which can make its wearer stand out as the acme of elegance even in a setting as sophisticatedly mundane, as dramatically foreign and foreignly domestic, as stepping out of a hotel into a hired car, bag swinging free, a comment tossed backward over the shoulder like a scarf toward the panting belaboring suitcase-beladened male who momentarily pauses before the loading of the car (the beloved having popped back into the hotel as nimbly as Ariel escaping into the wings), like a man contemplating a combined problem-solving exercise and test of leadership in the face of an army officer selection panel: These planks, this rope, these men, that ravine, now how do you build a bridge across?

Allowing one peach per person, dip the fruit into boiling water for thirty seconds before peeling and stoning them.

Give everyone a glass of red wine or Sauternes if you prefer (I prefer, I prefer). Dunk the sliced peaches. Sugar if taste so dictates—*de gustibus non est disputandum.*

"You said once that peaches remind you of your brother," my biographer remarked to me a while ago. I pretended not to be able to remember. The truth is that the furry fruit does indeed remind me of my sibling, thanks to an unfortunate event that occurred when we were both small: a near-fatal case of poisoning that resulted when I, in an early stab at culinary experimentation, prepared a jam made out of peaches and also out of peach stones—the latter containing, it turns out, cyanogen, a stable compound that, when broken down through contact with certain enzymes (or when, for instance, pounded up using a mortar-and-pestle), produces the celebrated toxin cyanide. The fruit was literally dropping off the trees that summer near our holiday cottage, falling from branch to ground with a "plop" that was so visible it was almost audible, and I was unable to resist an attempt at jam-making, the basic procedure for the manufacture of preserves having been taught to me by Mitthaug, who in the traditional manner of the northern kitchen was a scholar and aficionado of all forms of preserves, pickles, and condiments. My brother's stomach-upset, though acute—his fondness for peaches having already been noted—was (obviously) not fatal, though the *médecin,* a somber man with the air of concealed power and sadness belonging to an Angevin duke in bas-relief, had a worried forty-eight hours, as did my mother. No blame attached. For the record, it is not cyanide itself that smells of almonds, as portrayed in what has become a cliché of *noir* detective cinema, but flesh that has been poisoned by cyanide. A similar toxicity can be achieved with roasted apple seeds.

I remember once explaining to Bartholomew that the influence of Eastern art on that of the West—naturally I wasn't thinking about his own daubs and chiselings in this elevated context—could be compared to the introduction of Eastern plants and vegetables, whose effect has been far greater than any of the broader movements of history, wars, revolutions, mass migrations, etcetera. Consider, for example, the history of the peach, originally found in China, brought west by the Persians (hence its name, *Prunus persica,* though in one version it is Alexander the Great himself who tucked the fruit into his baggage chain along with his other plunder) before being brought farther west, into Europe "proper," by the Romans. To look into history is to look into the void. If one were to have a proper historical understanding of the potato, for instance, encompassing its origin in Peru, where its properties were so crucial to the highest civilization ever to have lived (highest in the sense of altitude) that the Inca's basic unit of time was predicated on how long it took to cook a potato; its arrival in Europe in the 1570s, where it became a dominant crop due to its ease of planting and cultivation, its high yield of carbohydrates and vitamins, its suitability to subsistence farming; the French resistance to the potato as a food for human beings, related to the widespread belief that potatoes caused leprosy; the way in which this belief was overcome by Antoine-Auguste Parmentier, who had acquired a taste for potato soup while in a Prussian prison and returned to make the tuber the flavor of the moment, so much so that potato-flowers began to be worn in the lapels of courtiers at the court of Louis XVI, the man behind this craze being commemorated to this day in the names of *potage Parmentier* and *crêpes Parmentier* (it seems that he may have hoped that the vegetable itself would come to be named after him; at a dinner for Benjamin Franklin, he designed a menu that featured potatoes in every course); on to the tuber's tragic apotheosis in nineteenth-century Ireland, where its various virtues caused it to establish a virtual monoculture, and thus to play a determining role in a famine that killed a million people—if one were genuinely to comprehend this history, then every bite of potato would taste of ash, and we would be unable to eat. But of course we do comprehend, more or less, and we go on eating just the same, just as the knowledge that a child dies of starvation or preventable disease somewhere in the world every few seconds has no effect whatsoever on our ability to bumble happily through our days. Forgetting these facts, ignoring them and distracting ourselves from them, is an essential act of civilized life. "Every act of civilization is also an act of barbarism"; a fact of which the potato reminds us; and a fact which the forgiving tuber then entices one sensuously to forget.

As I had anticipated, we spent the morning motoring westward into Brittany, into the landscape of inlets and coves and bays, where the cold-running water gushes through the *abers,* and flat tidal races try to penetrate the heart of France itself. A country with a predominance of inlets and coves will always have a feeling of insularity, of time lying heavily in silent country lanes where lives stand still among the wheat. Brittany can seem like a scale model of Cornwall made one and a half times larger, the sky bigger and wider, the stone walls and hedgerows rougher, the trees scarcer but also taller, the sense of the size and power of the Atlantic stronger. And the involuted Breton seashore also offers the vertiginous expansion of distances found in fractal mathematics: a full trip around its three thousand miles of coastline would be equivalent to an overland walk from Brest to Peking or Marrakesh to Durban. In a modern equivalent of Zeno's paradox, the closer the focus, the longer the distances appear to be.

We passed fields of beets and cows and, once, a startling uncovenanted field of lavender, its purple taking a second or two to register on the conscious mind, to bypass the neuronal resistance to its apparent impossibility. Once, leaving the cottage in Norfolk to return to London after a solitary but profitable weekend, I realized that I had forgotten some papers. I had locked up the house and switched off the lights but had not yet got into the car or turned on its lights. My reluctance to go back into the darkened house (cloud cover, no moon, interstellar blackness) grew rapidly, exponentially; I knew that I was frightened of seeing a ghost. But the fear contained in the idea was less of a ghost per se—after all, what power does a revenant have beyond and above the power of simply appearing? What further power does it need? It wasn't the idea of some elaborate horror-film denouement (the tottering mummy fulfilling an ancestral curse, the chain-saw-wielding asylum escapee)—no, it was the fear of seeing something that was impossible. That's why we're really frightened of ghosts: because they don't exist. So what would it mean if we saw one?

Brittany has an extensive tradition of supernatural law. I mean lore. The role played in it by ghosts is rivaled by that of omens and precognitions and warnings: there is no mythology anywhere that gives these anticipatory revenances as much prominence as do the Bretons. This is testimony to the Breton sense that the barriers between the dead and the living are permeable, an awareness that penetrates their entire culture with a sense of what can only be described as spookiness; and the awareness of premonition is of course curiously like that of neurotic anticipation, a feeling that imminent disaster is hiding expectantly behind the tattered arras of normality. The ancient Romans, who were also big on this kind of thing, must have lived in a permanent state of nervous crisis, fearing that every expedition out of doors might lead one to encounter some disastrous omen in the shape of a single raven, a glimpse of oneself in the wrong kind of reflective surface, or simply a cloud of the wrong shape moving at the wrong speed in the wrong direction. Perhaps, though, there are analogies between the psychic structures of precognition and those of art, which also depends on the accumulating effect of hints, glimpses, and the gradual accretion of that sense of foreboding which also goes by the name "meaning."

Death, then, gives Brittany its cultural distinctiveness. It is as if the trappings of Bretonness—the funny names;

the allegedly distinctive psychology which no outsider can in practice ever actually discern; the culinary peculiarities in terms of seafood, pancakes, and the absence of wine or serious cheeses; the glimpses of pan-Celtic affinity in the outcroppings of the original Breton language, all those Kers and Kars and Yanns, rising out of the limpid omnipresence of French like a reef in clear water, only to be given a parodic touristic quasi-life in token gestures like the double nomenclature of road signs—were a set of accidents, a set of properties hired from a costumier, designed to illustrate (but, if anything, serving to conceal) the fundamental and substantive truth of Bretonness, a sense of the proximity and nonirrevocability of all transactions between this world and the next. Only the image of death in Mexico (figure of color, of a comparable pre-Christian harshness, and of carnival—*carne levare,* farewell to flesh) is as vivid and as grotesquely alive as the half-comic, terrifying, grimacing skeleton figure of the Breton *Ankou.* And in both cultures, the energy with which death is celebrated and embodied is a tribute, a very pagan tribute, to the pressing presentness and thisness of life. To put it another way, has anyone anywhere in the history of the world ever genuinely believed in the reality of life after death? When Mitthaug fell in front of his train at Parsons Green station, was he telling himself that there would be more where this came from? One suspects not.

I hoisted the car onto a scraggly grass verge and walked the last few hundred yards toward the *enclos paroissial* of Kerneval. This is a classic example of the *enclos,* the church-statue-ossuary combination unique to Brittany. The first thing a visitor sees is the monumental entrance to the church square, a high arch supporting three smaller columnar arches above an elaborately carved balustrade. Running around the structure is a riotous profusion of carved figures representing, in chronological progression from left to right: Eve being born out of Adam's rib (Adam is bearded, peaceful; Eve is blank-visaged, and appears to be wearing plaits; a cow and a sheep, the beasts of the field, look on in apparent surprise); the destruction of Sodom and Gomorrah, or more specifically the flight of Lot and his family therefrom, symbolized in three figures of increasing size moving to the right and holding hands, while behind them sits an equivocal blob-like shape, presumably Mrs. Lot in the aftermath of her backward glance (the Old Testament again sparing us no details about how people really behave); Noah's Ark, a small tub-like vessel containing what appear to be a goat, a pig, a cow (again), and an out-of-scale elephant, as well as a headdress-wearing, crock-carrying shepherd figure, presumably Noah himself; moving on we have a convincingly triumphant and martial-looking Judith bearing aloft the head of Holofernes (whose eyes, like Adam's, are closed); a capering adult male, in front of a box being carried on poles by smaller men—conjecturally, David dancing before the Ark of the Covenant; and a stout female figure stooping over a fat little baby in a stone basket—Moses among the rushes, with washerwoman.

Beyond the portal—a triumphal arch of sorts—is a low-walled courtyard cum cemetery, leading to the church itself. On the left hunkered a squat granite building with an eaved roof; it wasn't difficult to identify the functional, threatening, memento mori look of the church's ossuary. This turned the enclosed space around the church into an area ruled by, under the sign of, dead ancestors. One would worship in the presence of their bones. The truth contained within that idea is of course that we carry our ancestors with us in our every gesture: Who has not caught himself performing an action as quotidian as picking up a glass, brushing the dust off a mantelpiece, only to realize with a start (one of the only things one ever does "with a start") that it is one's father, one's mother, whose tiniest gesture is being unconsciously but minutely reproduced? And perhaps the same applies to one's more extreme moments, and the grunt (or cry, or moan, or roar, or mew) one utters at the moment of ejaculation exactly mimics, is an unheard rhyme of, the noise made by one's father at the moment of one's own conception.

The church at Kerneval does not live up to the standard of its monumental archway. The proportions are subtly wrong. The steep angle of the roof and the rectangular massiveness of the walls conspire to fail to defy gravity; the statuary above the mullioned windows (which squat below the precipitous shelving) is not of the standard of the Old Testament narratives we have already discussed, partly because it tells no story—it is merely a series of New Testament characters armed with the emblems of their respective identities (Matthew's tax-collecting moneybag, Luke's painting instruments). "Stone never looks more like stone than when it's failing to look like something else," Bartholomew once remarked, *à propos* the distinctly unflowing robes of this statuary. In short, in this stonework the enlivening touch of the master is absent. Had he died, been sacked, got bored, or just walked away, taking his cloth bag of tools and his donkey and setting off, a pat from his familiar hand silencing his host's watch-dog as he parted stealthily and unfarewelled into the great upended bowl of the Breton night? My own art, also an affair of farewells and absences, resonates to the mystery of this.

I was reluctant, on this occasion, to enter the church. That morning, unable to decide which of my various wigs to put on, I had left it too late and settled simply on a charcoal-gray trilby hat. The battered, stylishly casual headgear—the sort of item worn in what used to be called Ealing comedies—was now resting with a not unpleasant sense of abrasion on my cool shaved scalp. Going into the church, however, would necessitate an act of respectful doffing that was naturally out of the question. Besides, they had gone in some time before me and would be liable to come out at any moment. In any case, the inside of the church is of no special interest, apart from an anachronisti-cally near-abstract tapestry depicting the victory of some count at some battle, and an overornamented altar covered with a hideous modern piece of sanctimonious-didactic embroidery—lambs lying down with lions, swords being beaten into plowshares, et cetera. Considered as a space, moreover, the interior of the church has the same deficiencies of proportion as the exterior ("It would, wouldn't it," as my brother used to enjoy saying, often aptly but still with a mysterious frequency). It lacked awareness of the basic laws of structure. For myself, I learned all I needed to know about the rules of proportion from the dry martini. (The addition of an onion turns this martini into a Gibson. Cocktail titles proliferate like ranks in the Ruritanian army.) The law is: main ingredient (gin), subordinate ingredient (vermouth), and grace note (lemon twist, olive). This is the law of proportion and rhythm that underlies all of the plastic arts, from cocktail-making and cooking to architecture, sculpture, pottery, and dressmaking. Remember where you heard it first.

It wasn't intelligent to keep standing there in the portal. I decided to adjourn for lunch. Across from the *enclos* stood a hotel outside of which six tables had sprouted *pastis*-advertising parasols like giant mutant fungi responding to the July sunshine. (One of the pleasures of civilized travel is the detection of future dining spots. Aha! one tells oneself. *There* shall my needs be gratified.) On my way over I dodged an asthmatic Mercedes whose driver, possibly not long for this world, was going the wrong way around the square while his bottle-blonde wife scowled over a *guide vert.*

It is possible to be oversentimental about French cooking. At the highest level there is no disputing that it is not so much capable of excesses as that it primarily consists of them. A dish such as *volaille truffée au beurre d'asperge à la crème de patate "Elysée Palace"* exists in a realm that has managed to exceed the wildest imaginable reach of parody—these dishes are the product of febrile imaginations in big white hats. Nonetheless, there is a level of ordinary culinary competence in France that is unsurpassed by any country of my acquaintance; it is a competence that manifests itself as a sensuous science of ordinary life, the application of intelligence to pleasure. Pierre and Jean-Luc, my rustic neighbors, would only ever talk freely—in a dignified, clipped, precise, engineer-like way—when discussing technical aspects of cooking, and it is to Pierre that I owe certain specifics of my gastronomic armamentarium, such as the correct method for steeping tripe, or which of the songbirds that the two brothers used to slaughter with their terrible blunderbusses had edible brains, or my knowledge of the liaising properties of rabbit's blood. Mrs. Willoughby, the neighbor who used to pop over uninvited to avail herself of my swimming pool, once popped over uninvited while Pierre and I were draining a freshly decapitated rabbit into a wide-mouthed stone jug that I bought from a dungareed female potter in the Saturday market at Cavaillon; Mrs. Willoughby had to run (again continuing the motif of uninvitedness) into the *cabinet de toilettes,* whence we could hear the unmistakable sound of large-scale vomiting.

One of the practical consequences of this Cartesian-evolved hedonism (I say Cartesian because the French attitude to pleasure is not that of a totally unified, whole-man, Epicurean/aesthetic attitude to the self, such as one might find on some idealized South Sea island; rather it is the product of a profound acceptance of the split between body and mind: it says, yes, my mind and my body are completely separate, so I must apply the full power of my mind to deriving the maximum possible benefit from the ownership of a body—nothing is more profoundly accepting of man as a dualistic entity than a precisely cooked *poulet à l'estragon*) is that the French take two hours off for lunch and their set menus are often a very good value. The *prix fixe* at the Hôtel Kerneval offered, for 75 francs, a choice of solid bourgeois cooking—terrines, pâté, *céleri remoulade, moules marinières, gigot d'agneau,* horse steak, *brandade de morue,* half a grilled lobster (50F *supplément*), fruit, cheese, *crème au caramel, mousse au chocolat, crème brûlée.* I had gently to insist to the bashful, prettily blushing waitress (showing clear signs of being alarmed and impressed by my perfect French) on a table with a view across the *enclos* and the parked cars in front of it.

I ordered watercress soup, grilled lemon sole, and—Brittany not producing any wine of its own and cider being a little too rustic for my mellow noonday temper—a spinsterish half-bottle of Menetou-Salon, with a liter of mineral water *du pays* (in an air-sea-rescue-beacon-red bottle) to wash it down.

A young couple came out of the church hand in hand and headed in the direction of the ossuary.

The watercress soup, becomingly served, had the transformedly rich texture that it sometimes achieves. There is a category of soup that attains a robustness one doesn't expect, a density of flavor and often of texture—almond soup, pea soup, lovage soup, etcetera. These soups are like those works of art (I am not specifically thinking about my brother's) in which a filigreed delicacy of local detail adds up to an agglomerated solidity of effect.

The hotel's restaurant had largely filled up by now. At the next table an elegant leather-trousered couple of, to judge by their BMW's license plate, Parisians, not in the *very* first flush of youth, his Gucci handbag slightly larger than hers, were debating as to whether or not to have the lobster. The waitress's blush had become, with the press of business, a flush of exertion, prettily tempering the fairness of her blond person's Norman skin, a color one sees on girls cycling home from school near the cottage in Norfolk.

The young couple had moved over to the monumental arch, still hand in hand, scrutinizing the statuary. She was doing most of the talking.

Lemon sole is, I think, an underrated fish, much closer in quality to its more highly regarded Dover cousin than received wisdom ordinarily permits—though this example of the species had had its unimpeachable freshness compromised by a degree of inaccuracy in the grilling. The sole was accompanied by some excellent *frites;* an acceptable green salad was served afterward. Clouds, which had been moving briskly across the sky all morning, were now beginning to coagulate and cast a cooling shade for fives and tens of minutes at a time. Pointing out cloud shapes used to be a favorite activity of my mother's, when she was having one of her attacks of being The Best Mother In The World. Look, a horse. Look, an antelope. A cantaloupe. A *loup-garou*. A *loup de mer*. A *sale voyeur*. A *hypocrite lecteur*.

I followed the sole with a *crème brûlée*. This, in the form of a dish called burnt cream, was originally an English pudding, though of course the custard is a Europe-wide phenomenon—the quiche, for instance, being a savory custard, and a recipe for "pan cheese" being available from the first-century A.D. writer Apicius. I told my collaborator, with that mixture of endearment and melancholy that attends the recitation of the follies of one's youth (not *all* that long ago, I should say), about something I did once in what I used to call my aesthetic period. The idea, cribbed from Huysmans, was to serve a menu consisting entirely of black things. This occurred during my brief interval at university, whence I departed after two terms (the *noise,* dear, and the *people*). My room, a banal heptagon in a banal heptagon-shaped building in one of the smarter Cambridge colleges, I had painted (slightly in violation of one or two of the more invasive college regulations) black. Bed, sheets, fittings, lamps, light bulbs—all black.

"I stayed in a chi-chi hotel in New York that was a bit like that," interrupted my interlocutor, with the headstrong impetuosity that accompanies relative lack of years and does not necessarily, all appearances to the contrary, indicate a lack of respect for the other party, rather a too active interest in him, foaming over momentarily like a milk pan left on at full roaring heat. "It was so trendy that, even after you turned the light on, you still couldn't see."

In my black room, dressed in black velvet, black silk cravat—no need to change the inherent color of the single orchid in my buttonhole—I would arrange for meals consisting entirely of black food: truffles grated over squid-ink pasta, followed by *boudin noir* on a bed of fried black radicchio. For dessert, I wanted to emphasize the essential artificiality of the event, the fact that it was a celebration of art, whim, caprice, set over against the brutal facts of nature and death, so I served crème brûlée, dyed black. Naturally we drank Black Velvet, that very English confection, combining clubmanly propriety with ninetiesish, Café Royalish institutionalized aestheticism, to which my father had introduced me, in his handsome way, in a hotel bar—the Shelbourne? the Gresham?—in Dublin, my father preempting the traditional imprecation "waste of good Guinness" by insisting on the drink being made with Courage's Imperial Russian Stout, difficult to get, rich, thick, sweet, as if it embodied that *douceur de la vie* which Talleyrand said no one who had not lived before the French Revolution had ever tasted. (Talleyrand used to spend an hour a day talking to his chef, who at one point was the incomparable Carême. When the great diplomatist warned the great cook of the dangers of coal-fired stoves, the betoqued genius replied, definitively for all members of the creative trades: "Shorter life, longer fame.")

Into this exquisite setting arrived Bartholomew, an hour and a half late, coming straight from his studio in his overalls (in violation of the dress code I had specified) and saying:

"Bloody hell! Anybody dead?"

That note of self-consciously deflating plain-man-speaks realism, the forthright expression of too direct opinion, was typical of my brother. There was a certain literalness to him, a lack of sensitivity to nuance, a coarse-grained practical achievingness that was apparent also in his sculpture (though none of the critics seems ever to have noticed it), less in the texture or grain of his work (though perhaps there a bit, too, to the more discerning eye) than in the very fact of that work's existence. As I have said before, there is something stupidly literal, something blindly, heedlessly forgetting, something of the bland imperturbable pleasure in crudeness of a police-man taking a visitor on a tour of famous murder sites, about any finished work of art. To put it another way, although Shakespeare's Prospero—wise, tired, unskepti-cal, full of power—is taken as being his creator's spokesman, perhaps his most accurate self-portrait is to be found in the bitter, maimed, deformed, unstoppable poet Caliban.

As it happens, the little Breton town of Kerneval in which I was lunching (in which, if you are prepared to succumb for a moment to the always fashionable illusion of the historic present, I am lunching, though in fact I am dictating these words in a Lorient hotel room where the venetian blinds and the swaying yellow lamp outside my window are flickeringly combining as if in an experimen-

tal attempt to induce an attack of *petit mal*) has some of
the rough-and-ready paintings my brother knocked off
during that period. This work comes from the time before
he began concentrating his efforts on sculpture. The
daubs are housed in a little local *musée de l'art contempo-
raine,* a chunky nineteenth-century building on the
enclosed side of the square which, oddly enough, by some
quixotic cocktail of local pride and misconstrued sense of
merit (the French being almost as notoriously erratic as
the Jack London–loving Russians when it comes to evalu-
ating the artistic products of the Anglophone world) is
named after my brother. One could almost imagine the
faction-fight at the *mairie:* the mayor's buddies caballing
over a *pastis* while his brother-in-law and sworn enemy,
the leader of the local Communist opposition, cooks up a
gerrymandering plan with his cronies over a jug of cider,
the resulting Mexican standoff in the badly ventilated
style pompier council hall building resulting in the com-
promise, to wit, the idea of naming the museum after
Bartholomew. The main exhibit of my brother's work
here, "inspired" by the archway of the *enclos*—and how
characteristically hubristic of my brother it was to pro-
claim himself to be modeling his work on something so
manifestly superior in scale, accomplishment, *finality* of
achievement—was a series of paintings depicting the
apostles and evangelists, not through direct portraiture
but through their identificatory tokens, duly updated:
Peter's fishing net, Luke's paintbrushes, Matthew's calculating machine, John's whatever, all having the air of

impulsively cast-off burdens, embodying the way in which the disciples had cast aside their previous lives when they set out to follow Christ.

Our young couple came out of the museum and walked back across toward the archway for a final look at it. At a distance the arch looked writhingly alive, sentient, as if a moment of real life had been instantaneously preserved under a Vesuvian rain of ash, a representation of architecture less as frozen music than as solid cinema. They walked around the edge of the square toward their car, keeping to the marginal area of pavement that was so narrow and wall-hugging that it seemed to be apologizing to any inconvenienced motorists for its very existence.

A Luncheon on the Theme of Curry

The role of curry in contemporary English life is often misunderstood. It (curry, that is, not contemporary English life) is often seen as an exercise in what the French would call *le style rétro*. (The French are dedicated to slang as a means of systematizing the process of inclusion and exclusion, not crudely but in those small ways which cumulatively serve the function of telling the outsider that he doesn't quite get the point—making him suffer the tiny inner defeat of not understanding a punchline, not twigging a reference; as for instance the hotelier in this decent Lorient establishment—three-starred and restaurant-rosetted, some hundred-plus kilometers from the site of our luncheon, a distance achieved thanks to the excellence of the *route nationale* system in preference to the thronged competitive death-dealing surprisingly expensive autoroutes, and also thanks to the liveliness of my light Renault, not to mention the weather, the breeze racing over one's unreluctantly discarded trilby, the pattern of sunlight changing over the wind-darkened fields like the soul of man responding to the promptings of God— the hotelier used the word "*resto*" in an attempt to outflank my command of the colloquial; as I replied "*Oui, un bon resto*" I poker-playerishly detected in his eyes the momentary flicker of an unexpected reverse.) On this view, curry plays a nostalgic, retrogressive role in British culinary culture; the proliferation of restaurants specializing in it is a consolation prize for the loss of world-historical consequence; we are to be understood as having given away the Empire and received in return, in delayed settlement of that very considerable invoice, the street-corner tandoori house.

Nothing could be further from the truth. If there is a central theme to the historical appetite of the English it is a fondness for spices and for spicy food; the national desire for these enhancements of flavor and stimulants to the palate amounts to a millennium-long binge. Consider Carême's observation, at the time of his arrival at the court of the Prince Regent, that the use of spices was so emphatic that "the prince often had pains lasting all day and all night." One might go so far as to say that a taste for spices is an ingredient (!) of the national character, an instinct comparable to the Welsh talent for singing, the German liking for forests, the Swiss knack for hotel-keeping, the Italian passion for motor-cars. Spiced bacon, Barbados ham, pepper steak, spiced meat loaf, paprika cabbage—the English infatuation with spices runs through our history like a melodic undercurrent, or like the percussive backbone against which the daily music of time and the kitchen soars and twitters. Thus the records of English spice consumption show a heroic commitment to (especially) overrated cinnamon; the even more overrated, not far short of actively nasty clove; tasty soporific nutmeg and its sibling mace; aromatic allspice; flashy paprika; historic mustard seed; popular ginger; chili (which it must never be forgotten arrived in Europe some time before the Portuguese carried it to India, where the fiery pod was to have some of its most culinarily notable effects); warm-tasting, personal favorite, beds-i'-the-East-are-soft cumin; evocatively Middle Eastern coriander (its Greek etymology, from *koris,* commemorating the fact that it smells identical to the humble bedbug); risky cardamom; unmistakable caraway; lurid turmeric—I could go on.

It is often erroneously asserted that this enthusiasm for spices has its origins in a desire to disguise or conceal the degraded quality of the available produce—specifically, to conceal the corruption of spoiled meat. This is terribly evil and mad. The dominant theme in English cuisine is the use of spices for their own sake, especially in pursuit of effects that—and this is the real key to the historic national palate—combine the sour and the sweet. From the date of the amalgamation of the Sopers Lane Pepperers and the Cheap Spicers in 1345, to the commercial launch of Worcestershire sauce in 1838, and even more so thereafter, English eating is dominated by the pursuit of sweet and sour tastes together; national specialities such as the practice of serving mint sauce with lamb— regarded by the French as an incomprehensible perversion, closely linked to the national tastes for flagellation and cryptic crosswords—reflect that truth. The contemporary passion for violent combinations such as the sweet-and-sour dishes served in Chinese restaurants (and regarded unashamedly as *lupsup* or garbage by the Cantonese themselves) is no spasm of colonial nostalgia but the vigorous continuation of a pre-yeomanly appetite, more representative of historical continuity than any nonsense to do with beefeaters, cricket, the Book of Common Prayer, or the last night of the proms.

The same taste is also at work in the national passion for proprietary brands of sauces, ketchups, yeast extracts, et cetera, often loud in color and comparably unsubtle in taste, of which my brother was such a devout enthusiast. These concoctions are always to be found grouped in serried ranks, attentive, expectant, and shiny as toy soldiers, on the shelves of grocers' shops, and on the tables of workingmen's cafeterias of the type frequented by Bartholomew, the bottles clustering around the ketchup-bearing plastic tomato, still dented from the powerful finger-grip of the last customer.

I remember making these or similar points, as usual with an attractive air of qualified omniscience, to my collaborator. We were dining in a high-grade Indian restaurant (linen, silver) in the capital; myself fresh down from Norfolk, she naturally vacating her schedule to make time to see me. Negotiations and discussions were at an early stage, and I wanted to dine in public as a way of theatricalizing the occasion and of making it seem—in the paradoxical way of public spaces, and according to the thermodynamic law of coupledom advanced earlier, whereby a meal eaten in public always constitutes either an advance or a retreat in a relationship, never a steady state—more intimate. The restaurant's atmosphere of Establishment solidity, the calm authority of its heavy furnishings, had a club-like air; on the first floor, its long-windowed main room and grave Tamil waiters spoke of permanences and of the mystically enduring distillates of Empire.

What did we discuss? The weather, the similar quality of light in towns favored by painters in the South of France and Cornwall (Collioure, St. Ives), curry recipes, why people like to read biographies, the fallacy of the idea of the biographical fallacy, *In Praise of Folly,* a shared addiction to antique shops, the use of imposters in the fiction of P. G. Wodehouse, the architecture of Sir John Soane, how boring we both found the idea of the "English eccentric," the fashion in women's clothes for something she called "ra-ra skirts," which I said seemed to me to be a deliberately less flattering amendment of the tutu.

Our starters (strangely literal term: one doesn't call pudding "finishers"; on the other hand, who truly deserves their dessert?) we fetched for ourselves from the opulent buffet. I chose an agreeably crisp aubergine *bhaji,* a well-judged dab of cucumber *raita,* a *poppadum.*

"When I was a kid I used to be scared of Indian restaurants because I thought you had to eat puppy dogs," confided my companion.

"I have only ever eaten dog once, in the course of an experimental and unrepeated visit to Macao. One had won rather spectacularly at roulette and wanted to commemorate the event with a meal to remember. One celebrated afterward with a bottle of Krug and a puppy casserole. Not a success, overall—somehow both stringy and fatty. Served in a big sort of cauldron, not unlike the kind of thing you tend to see in productions of *Macbeth.* 'It tasted like chicken.' The stir-fried vegetables were the best thing about the meal, something you often find in not absolutely first-rate Cantonese restaurants. The Cantonese call that quality of precise stir-frying 'wok fragrance.' "

"I couldn't eat dog. I'd throw up."

"J'aime les sensations fortes."

We followed with a Bengal fish curry made with hake and a little too much turmeric (for him) and a charcoal-baked quail or rather quails, nicely executed with a blackened coat of spice, served on its somehow compulsory but profoundly un-Indian accompaniment of shredded lettuce (for her).

The quail made me think of Pierre.

"I have this little place in Provence—nothing spectacular, hardly much more than a hut really. One summers there. One's neighbors (this naturally being long before the English infestation of the past decade or so) are a charming pair of brothers, so rustic, so simple, so *echt* Provençal—luckily one has a smattering of the local dialect from one's readings in Cavalcanti. One or other of them will sometimes bring 'round something he has caught or shot; once I remember Pierre brought a brace of songbirds, only a little smaller than that quail there. I'll never forget the way he eviscerated them with one scooping movement of his hand and then pressed them flat with the other, pushing down on top of them with the palms of his hands, like so—crunch. Instant spatchcocking. I popped them into a marinade for an hour or two. Simply grilled over charcoal—*magnifique.* Though it was always a source of wonder to me that the brothers ever advertently managed to kill anything."

"Was food a big thing for your brother? Was he very interested?"

I always associate her with the sensation of light, the unpredicted arrival of quantities of light—through wind-dancing branches, or angling into a room like Zeus disguised as a sunbeam to seduce Danaë.

"I'm not sure how interested we should be in the idea of interest. It's such a secular category of mental activity—it implies such an emptying out of content. One can't imagine Dante or Pascal being 'interested' in something. Pascal's 'interest' in roulette was a terrifying confrontation with the omnipresent immanence of his creator, a face-to-face interview with God. You would no more ask him if it was 'interesting' than you would ask a matador if he was 'interested' in bulls, a man in a crow's nest on a windjammer during a gale whether he was 'interested' in reefs, a ballet dancer at the apogee of his leap whether he is 'interested' in gravity, a whore checking the balance of her savings account whether she is 'interested' in men. It's a condition of our banality that we are so interested in things; that we assume that the idea of interest has any force. None of the most important events in our life is 'interesting'—birth, copulation, death. A man standing on the edge of the abyss has passed beyond interest in the void. *Abyssum abyssum vocat.* My brother had no interests in that debased but admittedly functional sense of the term, but he did have a great fondness for proprietary sauces and ketchups. He took a large box of HP sauce with him when he went to live in Brittany. Perhaps it would after all be fairer to describe this as a passion than as an interest. It certainly used to distress our mother, though she would pretend to be amused when he drenched his *oeufs sur le plat* (so infinitely superior to our own fried egg, as I hope I shall have the pleasure of demonstrating to you one morning) in pungent brown modificator. He loved the pickles made by our Norwegian cook, and I once personally witnessed his eating an entire quart jar of Mitthaug's cocktail onions, which were so good that it was a regular family joke to suggest that he should set up a business dedicated to their manufacture."

"I suppose he was usually too busy to cook."

"Tink tink tink tink tink tink tonk tonk tock. His chisel was never far from hand. Though he used to turn his hand to stews and daubes and the like in a rough-and-ready, male kind of a way. One of our servants, an Irishwoman, taught him to make an acceptable Irish stew. He started to make it at around the time he was becoming increasingly committed to sculpture in preference to painting. One of his landlords tried to sue him for causing structural damage to the house because of all the stone he had dragged up to the loft. There would be a procession of block-heaving sweating laborers, hefting impossible weights up precipitous stairs, as in a domestic reenaction of the construction of the Pyramids, the whole scene permeated with the smell of simmering lamb. I notice on this menu here they list a spicy version of Irish stew, as adapted to suit the palates of the Christian Brothers in Madras."

"You don't remember the name of the landlord who tried to sue him?"

"Indeed Anglo-Indian cooking is, in general, a neglected but fascinating subject."

The role played by spices in general, and by curry in particular, in my own cooking is not small, I went on to explain. (To this extent, the account given earlier of the national affinity for sharply flavored food is a self-description. Perhaps all description is self-description, and every word we utter is merely a fragment toward an autobiography of our bodies, our consciousnesses, its full pattern discernible, like the desert lines at Nazca, only by an observer whose position and motive strain our imaginations to envisage—UFO landing-pad guide marks? Colossal astronomical calendars? Keats: "A man's life of any worth is a continual allegory." Discuss.) Though I should put in a demurral to the effect that my taste is for the lighter, more vivid palette of Oriental flavors, rather than the heavier, "gloppier" curries and sauces so prevalent in the transplanted Eastern cuisines now to be found in this country. The texture of the standard curry-house version of what has become Britain's national dish owes much to the techniques of its composition, involving a standard sauce which is subsequently amended by modifying agents of a varying toxicity: standard glop + vindaloo gunk = finished dish. One might further note that almost every "Indian" restaurant in the country is in fact owned and run by Sylhetis, people from the eponymous landlocked province in up-country Bengal; it is as if every "European" restaurant in the world were to be staffed exclusively by émigré Andorrans.

My own curries are more vivid, more instinct with that sense of hard-edgedness and distinction between objects so characteristic of the real (as opposed to the imagined and Orientalized) East. For treats and on special occasions I will prepare a *kurma,* the mild curry whose use of sour curds gives it a quality of appeasing spiciness; this needs to be cooked twice, once before and once after the addition of the unstable and potentially treacherous yogurt—so it is, as my young friend observed of my well-nigh-professional-standard onion-chopping technique, "a bit fiddly." On feast days and bonfire nights I have been known to rustle up a *pilaf* or *biryani,* the stimulatingly diverse flavorings of the rice combining with the heavy or delicate qualities of the accompanying curry—a combination made especially festive by the traditionally auspicious accompaniment of gold-leaf topping, though I should record that I myself have never, notwithstanding the medical properties gold has historically been said to possess, found the edible applications for the fickle metal (an authorized additive under European law, incidentally, allocated the intoxicatingly boring number of EU permitted additive E175) to be anything other than disappointing. Both of these dishes are of Moghul origin, creations of the pale-skinned Aryan conquerors from the north, their role as conqueror-civilizers so similar to that of the Normans in England. My brother had a gold goblet given to him as a token of esteem by some overexcited benefactor or other, which he, in my view oikishly even by his standards, used to keep paintbrushes in. All that glitters is not E175.

Our menu consists of

Egg Curry
Prawn Curry
Condiments
Mango Sorbet

The principle behind the combination is that the prawn dish is sharp and hot and stimulating, while the egg dish is mild, sour, and soporific. The mango sorbet adds welcome notes of sweetness, coolness, and acidity, and the meal has the overall singleness of purpose and effect within a unifying framework of diverse energies that is generally taken to be, but is not exclusively, the property of the great statements of the classical cuisines of the West.

In preparing the condiments bear in mind that the most effective way of subduing chili-heat in food is through starchy and cool things—rice, potatoes, bananas, beer, yogurt—instead of through neutral and noninterventionist water. As to the mango sorbet, you should 1) buy a sorbetière, 2) buy some mangoes, 3) follow the instructions. The curry recipes you can look up in a book. Bear in mind that the practice of "deveining" prawns—breaking open their backs with a surgical forefinger or a knife, and stripping out the dark thread of the alimentary canal—is necessary only in the tropical climates where food "goes off" quickly (like people, or like a linen suit on a muggy afternoon), though there it is very necessary indeed, unless it is your specific intention to poison somebody.

"Perhaps I will prepare it for you one day," I flirtatiously concluded after describing the curry luncheon outlined above, while also sexily raising the last of a ripe papaya, God's improvement on the melon, to my eager lips. At other tables around the restaurant waiters cleared, swept, shuffled, arranged, surgeons or looters attending the ruined battlefield of lunch.

"I'd like that. Did you often cook that for your brother?"

"It was a particular favorite of Bartholomew's—a meal which I must have rustled up for him in half a dozen different settings, comfortably in Norfolk, improvisedly in Provence, once safari-like in his festering studio in New York, me always arriving, as a special fraternal treat, with small packets of spice crimped in paper in a delabeled coffee jar whose original identity was still discernible from the color and helpfully polygonal shape of the lid; he would always consume depressing amounts of industrial chutney."

Curry was perhaps one of the things Bartholomew came to miss when he lived in France. I have had cause to ruminate on these matters in the course of this very evening in Lorient, where the smell of the sea can just be perceived in the lightening breeze. The meal in my hotel restaurant was expensive, overambitious, and marred by the insufficiently theorized use of spice to which the French are prone. (Only in the already mentioned *curry d'agneau* at La Coupole have I encountered a full comprehension of *les épices*.) Here, the offending dish was a botched amalgam of spices with allegedly fresh seafood (scallops, langoustines, gristly periwinkles, and a pongy oyster or two)—though one notes that the affinity between shellfish and cumin was known as far back as Apicius. At about the same time a favored occupation of high-caste Romans was to buy a large fresh red mullet, invite some friends around for the evening, remove the fish from its tank of water, and relishingly and languorously watch its color change and modulate (red, orange, cinnamon, mauve, gray, silver) as it died. This pastime, while commendably decadent and pretentious, and bracingly instrumental in its approach to our planet's other species, still (in common with other practices of the Romans) has the power to strike the contemporary observer as a bit *much.*

After dinner I broke into a room on the floor below mine. I have always found the technique of opening a Yale-locked door with a credit card to be perceptibly, even comically, more difficult than it is depicted in films and on television, and I was pleased to see that the *Mossad Manual of Surveillance Techniques* (*not* available in a bookshop near you, though obtainable in photocopied form from small mail-order advertisements in the more paranoid mercenary periodical literature) simply recommends the procurement (which may in practice mean the purchase from some concierge or janitor figure) of a set of master keys.

The room's furniture was identical to that of my own—tasteful bureau here, mini-bar disguised as a teak cabinet there—though it was, I noticed, slightly larger, for, as I discovered on checking the *tarifs,* the same price. A large boastful male leather suitcase bestrode a folded-out wooden stand, while a smaller, tidier, stiff-sided brown female case lay open on the bed, the one or two smarter dresses already intelligently hung in the armoire. I glimpsed a suggestive mulch of clean underthings in the yawning sexual gulf of the spread-eagled bag. Time, however, pressed. I slid my hand into one of the suitcases and extracted a large packet of travel documents, the principal one for which I was searching—a handwritten itinerary—being helpfully on top. It was the work of a moment to copy the relevant dates, times, and bookings into my little moleskin notebook before assiduously reassembling the documentation and popping it back where I had found it. The tall narrow overdesigned lamp on the bedside table (next to an exploding wallet of hotel information, tourist leaflets, and stationery) was plugged underneath the bed into a standard continental three-plug two-pointer, which I deftly exchanged for an only slightly fatter-looking unit of my own before exiting the room with a final regretful glance and an efficient once-over for signs of intrusion.

Time for a drinky-poo. I was told by the waiter, his manner bulging with concealed traditional merriment at the thought of the honeymooners' activities, that the English couple (in fact 50 percent Welsh, though I naturally resisted the temptation to put him straight on the point) had slyly snuck into town for a cheaper and better meal at some unheralded crêperie, and were expected back in a half hour or so. I digested the information with the help of a fruity young Calvados. Then I sauntered upstairs, disdaining the lift (to the horror of the staff) and pausing only to sneer at a couple of scenic watercolors, understandably tucked away on the landing. A street lamp was casting a smear of sodium-colored light over my bedstead, another reason to be irritated about the price of the room.

I waited for three-quarters of an hour and then, at five minutes past ten, took out the receiver, a bulky object about the size of the Penguin edition of *Mastering the Art of French Cooking,* its earphones already plugged into it. The frequency had been preset ("It's modeled on baby alarms," the man in the shop—so badly cut shaving that he looked like the perpetrator of an insincere suicide attempt—had told me).

"And you don't necessarily find out things about him by looking at his work," an immediately dislikable male voice was saying.

"I've been bitten. Why is it always me who gets bitten?" There was bathroom activity. "And I never said that they did tell you things about him. And it's not the other way around, either. It's just that it's interesting to see the stuff in the places where he made it, especially as in some cases they're the places he made it for. Anyway you knew what you were taking on when you took me on. I'm sorry if it seems like a waste of a honeymoon. Don't touch me, I'd rather scratch my bites."

There were the noises of silent reconciliation, of shufflings around the room, taps, suitcases, drawers. Then there were other sounds.

· Summer ·

General Reflections

An *Apéritif*

Vegetables and Saladings

A Selection of Cold Cuts

General Reflections

In the summer, the intelligent cook is likely to find that the formally structured menu has less of a role to play. The constraints of the other seasons, imposed in the form of closed doors, draft-barred windows, and securely buttoned clothing, are eased, and with those relaxations comes a sense of psychic liberation comparable to the summertime freedoms extended to children in poor Mitthaug's native Scandinavia, where even the very notion of bedtime is abandoned in the face of night-long daylight, and in the knowledge that winter restores a punitive equilibrium of unending dark. Of course, the sense of increased liberty can bring a paradoxical sense of oppression, a feeling of "I must be having a good time—am I having a good enough time—I'm not relaxing—I'm too tense—I wish I could try harder to relax—I must enjoy myself. . . ." I thought I could detect one or two symptoms of this in the female half of the young couple, flagrant honeymooners, whom I observed the next morning across the distinctly uncrowded breakfast room, via a tiny hole in my copy of *Le Monde* that I had drilled with a hot compass and then widened with a twirled fountain pen and a judicious index finger. The room's bad oil paintings synesthetically mimicked the slight rankness of the stale coffee, served in those pretentiously unpretentious big French bowls.

This section will not consist of rigidly articulated menus as such. Rather, if the menu can be compared to a sentence—in which individual syntactic units, nodes of energy, saber-thrusts, are connected by grammatical principles that link the units together, order and control the energy, choreograph and coordinate the individual moments of expression into a cohesive statement—then this chapter more closely resembles the individual lumps of psychic matter that precede the finished sentence. Instead of recipes and menus per se the reader will find suggestions for recipes, sparks flung from the wheel.

An Apéritif

Although *apéritif* is an evocative word—in itself containing a vivid image of *luxe, calme et volupté,* a sense of life spaciously lived—my own preferred term for the alcoholic beverage consumed at the end of the working day is "sundowner." The term points up the function of this drink, which serves to demarcate the conscious, wanting, achieving, workaday self from the relaxed, expansive, unbuttoned evening self; the moment of ingesting the sundowner being a liminal episode, a transition equivalent to that undergone by a shaman who has downed a rank quart of reindeer urine in which the hallucinogenic component of *Amanita muscaria* has been conveniently concentrated, and who, while not quite free of his quotidian awarenesses (the dirt, the rough skin of the totem animal abrasive on his hairy shoulders, the damp wood of the tribal fire smoking evilly into his watering eyes), is also not yet fully embarked on his voyage into alternative consciousness—the hurtling tunnel ride of psychic alterity. The end-of-day drink functions as the point at which one exchanges personae; one reason why, as the conventional wisdom has it, "a workaholic is the opposite of an alcoholic." Though as it happens my brother was both, unable to stop himself from putting in monstrous hours in his series of studios—and when I say the word "studio" I see a floating ballet of stone dust dancing in a lit atelier—with various mistresses telling identical stories of him having to be literally dragged away from his plinth and chisels; at the same time any cessation of work would immediately precipitate a one-man pandemic of drinking, as he powered undiscriminatingly through an inordinate amount of whatever was the local *vin-de-pays,* his alcoholic career thus encompassing absinthe binges in Marseilles, Calvados-fueled outrages in the Cherbourg hinterland, cider orgies not far from our hotel here in Lorient, *arrack* benders in Cappadocia, a period of *brennevín* abuse when researching geological formations from a clapboard house a few miles outside of Reykjavik, one-man red-wine bacchanals more or less anywhere he ever lived in continental Europe, *genever*-chugging research trips to the Rijksmuseum, a bourbon-swigging junket to the American South which segued neatly into a three-month tequilathon in New

Mexico, a scrumpy-powered summer working with granite in Devon, whiskey-oriented Soho binges whenever he visited London, and of course a deep commitment to beer, which meant that at every pub within a fifteen-mile radius of the cottage in Norfolk he was either greeted like a long-lost brother or forbidden from setting so much as a toenail over the threshold. Indeed, one of his best-known works, *The Libation,* treats the theme of drinking, its image of a spilt goblet, the stone "sensuously evoking," "miraculously capturing" etc. etc. the slushing flow of the liquid, being too well known to describe here.

My own taste in apéritifs is classical. There is little point in pretending that any pre-dinner drink is ultimately preferable to champagne, that most inspired and inspirational of English inventions. (When I made a similar observation to my collaborator, in my sometimes slyly controversial way, she was startled: "What?" she exclaimed. In rebuttal I quoted Etherege's *The Man of Mode,* 1676, in praise of "sparkling Champagne," which "quickly recovers / Poor laughing lovers, / Makes us frolic and gay, and drowns all our sorrows." The key word here is "sparkling," which antedates any French reference to the wine's *pétillement.* The bubbles in champagne are induced by a secondary fermentation taking place in the bottle; the process that produces the fizz is therefore crucially dependent on bottle-stopping technology—and in this the English were world leaders, thanks to the fact that cork stoppers were already being used in bottled ale, while the wine-drinking French were still employing hemp plugs. Thus the English were wolfing down considerable quantities of sparkling champagne from the time of the Restoration onward, with the French not catching on until about fifty years later. Bottoms up.)

That said, champagne is not for every occasion, just as Mozart is not. If the evening is informal but food-oriented, a casual supper taken on the terrace of my house in St-Eustache for instance, my preferred sundowner (and here the term, as one surveys the still potent Provençal sun disappearing behind the olive, lavender, and vine-wreathed hills, seems especially apt) is a blanc-cassis, a drink for which poor Mrs. Willoughby used often to invite herself, when she wasn't inviting herself over to use the pool or for some other reason. She would arrive, clasping a largely symbolic wicker basket (she would in some moods claim to be gathering herbs or mushrooms), scarf knotted bizarrely at her throat, unattractively flushed and sweaty from climbing the path that led around the back of the hill, just as the evening was starting to turn comfortably in on itself.

"Ooh, that looks nice," she would say. "Lovely and pink," she would sometimes add, a weakness for the color pink being an infallible sign of the defective taste one associates with certain groups and individuals: the British working class, grand French restaurateurs, Indian street-poster designers, and God, whose fatal susceptibility for the color is so apparent in the most lavishly cinematic instances of his handiwork (sunsets, flamingos).

Mrs. Willoughby was, in fact, a walking anthology of bad taste, a serial offender against the higher orders of art and discrimination. In that sense she was a useful bench-mark, an unacknowledged legislator of mankind. Her theoretical love of all things French, which was matched only by her actual incompetence with all aspects of the language and culture, was rooted in a primal distaste for what she always—heavily stressing the adopted Cornish-ness she had assimilated from her late husband—called "the English." At the same time her Englishness was her own prime characteristic; or rather it came before and took precedence over all her other characteristics; it was a pri-mary essence from which all her other attributes emerged; it oozed from her every pore, like garlic after an *aïoli* binge. (The taste of garlic at its most intense, chopped and uncooked, is detectable on the skin for up to seventy-two hours after ingestion. Recipe to follow.) So her lucubrations on the subject of the English—their small-mindedness and philistinism, their lack of culture, the ter-ribleness of their politicians, the dreadfulness of their past imperial misdeeds, the badness of their cooking, dirtiness of their cities, absence of significant artists in any of the century's major media, lack of clothes sense, dislike of bright colors, automatic contempt for anything they don't know about or don't understand, failure to learn foreign languages, instinctive conservatism, provincialism, and empiricism (I paraphrase slightly)—her denunciations, implicit and explicit, usually expressed in the form of chance remarks and small asides, served only to embody an impassioned and wholly unconscious self-dislike. This was apparent also in her wardrobe, which comprised an ensem-ble of fisherman's smocks, espadrilles (worn for the three-quarter-mile walk over rocky Provençal paths), and unseasonal berets, all of which added up to couturial suicide, with her essential Englishness and cluelessness never failing to shine through. There was something deeply appropriate and "ironic" about the way the *juge d'instruction* at her inquest, a pinched intelligent-looking man with an air of great weariness—as if he had ridden down from Paris on a succession of horses, without himself pausing for rest—kept referring to her as *la femme anglaise,* branding her for all time as the thing she least wanted to be but in actuality most was. As he described the technical details of the shotgun wound that had ended Mrs. Willoughby's life—the exit wound through the back of her head being an impressive eight centimeters in diameter, irrefutable testimony to the potency of Jean-Luc's blunderbuss, though it also brought that antique weapon into some suspicion as an instrument for killing birds or small game, since it would surely have reduced almost anything to a kind of gory raw lead-bearing pâté—the silence in the little courtroom had a depth and histrionic stillness so profound that, in the pauses between the learned magistrate's words, one could hear the heavy metallic ticking of the electric clock. Pierre and Jean-Luc sat in the front row of the room, immaculate and unfamiliar in their Sunday suits. Pierre, I could see out of the corner of one eye, was twisting in his hands a Harris tweed cap I had given him three Christmases before. My own explanation of the terrible misunderstanding that had taken place (Mrs. Willoughby having obviously misconstrued my strict instruction not to cross the brothers' property that particular day, as they had given me advance warning that they would be out shooting—it was as if she had disregarded the *pas* in a French sentence) was decisive. As the verdict of accidental death was passed Pierre and Jean-Luc turned and shook hands, the family resemblance never more present than in their shared expression of relief and suppressed triumph and an identical pungent sigh that only I was seated close enough to smell. There was something very moving about the simple dignity with which the brothers celebrated Jean-Luc's (let's face it) acquittal, their formal suiting and grave demeanor subsequently making them seem at ease amid the rigid napery of the local Michelin two-star, whose speciality is *alouettes rôties en croûte de sel, sauce madère.*

The general principles for apéritif-making are laid down in David Embury's *The Fine Art of Mixing Drinks,* one of the few books my brother was known to carry with him when he moved house, preferring to leave the bulk of his possessions behind him like a snake shedding a skin or a burglar making a getaway—and also a work which I on separate occasions heard him describe as "poncey" and "the best book ever written." Embury's general formulation is unimprovable. He states that an apéritif or cocktail 1) should be dry and cold, or at least should stimulate the appetite, as sweet and hot drinks do not; 2) should always keep the drinker intuitively apprised of how many drinks he has had, so that drunkenness does not creep up on him unanticipated, as it has been known to do with thick or eggy drinks. Martinis, daiquiris, and whiskey sours are acceptable cocktail alternatives to the classic French apéritifs; I personally find most Campari and vermouth libations to be disqualified by their innate nastiness of flavor (though thousands disagree); the anise-flavored drinks of the Mediterranean, Pernods and *ouzo*s and *arrack*s and *punt-e-mes,* are a different story. Gin and tonic is permissible. The manhattan is underrated. The use of scotch whiskey as opposed to bourbon in the manufacture of cocktails is forbidden. Calvados can only be used in the form of the sidecar, another now neglected former classic; though it is at its best taken neat, as by the workman standing next to me at the *zinc* where I found myself this very morning in Lorient, at a small *tabac* in a block of shops and apartments—the ground floor hosting two *tabacs,* a laundry, a pharmacy with a poster in the window listing different types of poisonous fungi, and a defeated seeming shoeshop. The last four of these enterprises were closed, unsurprisingly given that it was a quarter to seven in the morning (though the French in general go to work earlier than the English do).

Farther down the road, the habitable or human part of town came to an end, demarcated as abruptly as the front line in a classic trench war, in this instance perhaps the contest between man and commerce. There the industrial zone of town blossomed in a concrete and metal hundred-hectare parkland of warehouses and sidings; trucks were already loading, car parks filling, buses degorging. Across the street was the reason for my presence, the car rental establishment, *ouvert 0715 heures,* where I would be exchanging my Renault 5 for a speedy Peugeot 306 (the *Mossad Manual of Surveillance Techniques* recommends a daily change of pursuit vehicle).

The workman had on a pair of *les bleus de travail,* those heavy blue overalls which function as an unofficial uniform for the French manually laboring classes, and a heavy black moustache that seemed to be drawing the corners of his mouth and the pouches under his eyes downward as if in a protest against the forces of capital, of gaiety, of life itself; his hair, younger than the rest of him (dyed?), was combed forward like a Hollywood Roman's above a face still stiff with the earliness of the hour; he was breakfasting, in theory anyway, since he hardly seemed to be moving, the cigarette in the Pernod ashtray before him the only sign of volition or locomotive power, apart from a double espresso and a large *calva.* The heart trebly jolted.

"Encore une fois," I said with a slight courtierly inflection of the head down over my cup. The *patronne* removed the filter from the espresso machine, whacked it on the rim of the waste bin to void the exhausted grounds, twice clipped the ratchet at the bottom of the coffee grinder, and then tamped a new supply of coffee down into the filter with a twist of the wrist and the broad back of a dessert spoon—the first time she had used her left hand in the process—before slotting the ensemble back into the parent device and jabbing the button that compelled the heated and pressurized water to force through the mulch into the cup which she now, nick-of-timishly, cracked onto the drilled metal filter cum ledge below the mottled

metal spigot of the espresso machine, her movements throughout as abrupt and efficient and as angular as those of a clockwork automaton. I felt like bursting into applause. Instead, getting into the spirit of things, I simply used the mirror behind the *zinc* to adjust the angle of my display handkerchief. I still had half a croissant left.

Across the road a functionary of the car-rental company, tottering on the high heels of a particular type of overdressed French female office worker, unlocked the office and turned on the lights. The sudden internal illumination made the inside of the premises—a high counter, a computer terminal crouched on a desk—spring into visibility. I paid up (a nod from *Mme la patronne*) and crossed the road. A hundred yards away a rotary street-sweeping machine whined and strained as if preparing for takeoff. I would be back at the hotel before the honeymooners had even woken up.

Vegetables and Saladings

In Polish, the language of Poland, all green vegetables are known as *włoszczyzna,* which means "things Italian." The name is a tribute to Queen Bona Sforza, who had the good fortune to marry Sigismund in the sixteenth century and who as a result got the credit for introducing the produce of the southern garden to the freedom-loving people of her adopted country. More generally, the word *włoszczyzna* can stand as a tribute to the discrepancy between northern and southern attitudes to the produce of the garden, an archetypal Northerner being palely passionate about butter, beer, potatoes, and meat whereas his antithesis is enthusiastic about fruit and vegetables, oil and fish. (It might now be the occasion to remember that for the Romans, a barbarian was someone who wore trousers, had a beard, and ate butter.) The stereotypes do, however, have some basis in fact since, for large parts of the year, the produce of the northern kitchen garden is disappointingly narrow and unvaried and not at all well suited to the range of dishes made fashionable during the recent fad for all things Mediterranean (I should again stress here that I acquired my Provençal home long before this kind of thing became generally popular). Take the tomato for instance, a fruit whose exotic origins and nature are testified to by its very name, a derivation from the Nahuatl *tomatl,* and are unrelatedly but still stirringly present in its Latin classificatory name, *Lycopersicon esculentum,* "the edible wolf's peach." Surely its color, its lividity, must have reminded the Aztecs who ate it of the hearts they routinely saw ripped out at the daily human sacrifice? And in the defense of those onlookers, can it not be said that they at least personally witnessed the acts of cruelty on which their civilization rested? Uninsulated by the appropriately named media?

The tomato is available in every market and supermarket in the United Kingdom for twelve months of the year. For the overwhelming majority of that time it has no taste—none at all. Even the foreign-grown tomatoes on sale are close to absolute insipidity, the reason for this being that they are picked while still green and allowed to "ripen" in transit; I will never forget the expression on Mitthaug's face the first time (during an ordinary roadside picnic luncheon on a family expedition to Agen one August) he ate a fully ripe tomato—the expression of surprise and near-sensual shock was, even to my child's eyes, undisguisedly sexual. Etienne, the exchange student who stayed with us for a series of Augusts (to keep up my French after we had moved back to Blighty), was under strict instructions to bring the maximum possible number of ripe tomatoes; as a result he would struggle down the platform at Victoria with what looked like the entire contents of a market stall stashed into string bags. The tomato plant itself is toxic, though not sufficiently so to be of much use to the authentic poisoner.

Other vegetables are comparably underwhelming when eaten out of season. Take the sweet pepper, whose more potent (and, to this cook and eater, more stimulating and culinarily challenging) cousin the chili has already been discussed. The sweet pepper available in British shops all year round tastes like nothing so much as an ingenious new kind of high-technology plastic; it is exceeded in insipidity only by the sinisterly bland and anonymous iceberg lettuce, which outdoes all the competition by virtue of literally never having any taste at all—none whatsoever, ever; a perverse foodstuff that, if it had been created in a laboratory, would be an achievement of which any mad scientist could be legitimately proud. Conversely, there are other vegetables which are at their best in winter, like the celery which comes to its full livening glory in the depths of winter (*"morte saison, que les loups se vivent du vent,"* according to Villon) or its cousin the tragically underrated celeriac, or the leek, grown from Egypt to the far north of Scotland, mankind's friend in the hardest winter, and a known vegetable in England since the time of the Romans, being commemorated in place names as distinct as Loghrigg (*laukr,* Norse for "leek"— leek ridge) to Leighton Buzzard. In *Acetaria,* an excitingly semi-readable book about salads, for about three hundred years the only work on the subject in the English language, the diarist, antiquarian, and champion gossip John Evelyn described the leek as being "of Vertue Prolifick," and as a particular favorite of Latona, the mother of Apollo: "The Welch, who eat them much, are observ'd to be very fruitful." (I could forgive her many things, but his Welshness is hard to bear.) The excellent properties of the leek, however, are not available all the year 'round, and are confined to certain sections of the calendar. One of the few things that isn't, I suppose, is the fry-up breakfast so beloved of my brother.

Still, despite the powerful counterexamples of leeks and celery, it is indubitably true that the real nexus of vegetable quality arises in the summer, and that this season provides the cook with the prime opportunity for the presentation of the fruits of the garden in their simplest and (often) best form. The cook's mission is to bring the garden to the table. In practice this will tend to involve the construction of some form of salad. For most people raised in the U.K. there are few words in the language more likely to inspire a primitive and automatic loathing. "The salad is the glory of every French dinner and the disgrace of most in England"; this remark of the British traveler, Captain Ford, in 1846, holds as true as ever it did, in the assemblages that were created at my brother's aforementioned school St. Botolph's, for example—a few melancholy slices of cucumber, an approximately washed lettuce (iceberg, naturally), which appeared to have been shredded by wild dogs, two entire radish heads (served whole, presumably to avoid the risk of their proving edible in sliced form), a pale and watery quarter of tomato, the whole ensemble accompanied by a salad cream that at least had the virtue of tasting "like itself"—that's to say, like the byproduct of an industrial accident. Variations on this salad are eaten up and down the British Isles every day; one such salad is being eaten as I speak, another as you read. Perhaps the ancients were correct to regard lettuce as a soporific, and might have gone further, seeing it as a drug that induced an indifference to the form in which it was consumed.

This was one of the areas in which Mitthaug had to be most extensively coached and reeducated and deprogrammed. The experience of salad with which he came to us, his face beaming with what I know retrospectively to have been a compound of expectation and nerves and simulated eagerness, but which at the time seemed merely an uninhabited good-naturedness, was nugatory. The first mélanges he constructed for us were firmly at the nightmare end of the cold vegetable spectrum, a particularly unwelcome role being played by chunks of beetroot, "a vegetable for which," as my father remarked, "there is no excuse." My mother, a fastidious eater who preferred to avoid "hands-on" engagement in the kitchen, had to be conscripted to coach him through the principles of the assembled salad, starting with dressings. Mitthaug acquired these techniques faithfully, though there was still a sense of their being a dutifully learned set of techniques rather than a fully interiorized program; the absence of shredded lettuce and diced carrots could never be fully relied upon. "How can someone so good produce something so bad?" my mother would wonder, lifting a piece of wilted leaf between dainty fingers.

I had luncheon that day in the Relais de Pantagruel, a pretentious Loire restaurant a few hours' drive from Lorient in my shiny new Peugeot 306. The salad served at lunch would have shocked my mother as much as her creations used to alarm Mitthaug. I had ordered the *menu du jour* because I was eager to eat the main course specified on it, pike in a *beurre blanc,* that speciality of the Loire, indeed the nearest thing to a great classic dish in an area which is oddly (given its cultural, historic, and geographical centrality) short of contributions to the central canon of classic French cooking; pike being a good eating fish which English anglers tend not to bother with on account of its boniness (small, aggressive, sharp pointed bones they are, too, like fierce little toothpicks, the tiresomeness of picking them out being one of the reasons for the invention and success of *quenelles de brochet*), and *beurre blanc,* in addition, being celebrated for its particular affinity with this ferocious marauder of the lake depths. This was to be succeeded by a *tarte à la crème*—custard in pastry, or a crème brûlée in which the caramelized crunchy topping has been exchanged for a buttery, tarty base. The first course was to be a no-frills *pâté de campagne,* in which pork and prunes both played a role, and there was to be an "intermezzo" (their word) of *salade du chef*—which turned out to be a silent visual pandemonium of flowers and leaves, yellow and orange nasturtiums, white and red and pink rose petals, purple something blossoms, marigolds and lilies vying with each other in their yellowness, with *lollo rosso,* red chicory, and the dark, confident green of lamb's lettuce providing the tenor and bass notes. Black plates, alas. The use of flowers in cooking has always had an element of decadence, from Apicius's recipe for brains with rose petals in the first century A.D., through the herb-and-flower salads of the English baronial kitchen, to Marinetti's Futurist recipe for battered and deep-fried *rose diaboliche.* Marinetti especially recommends the recipe to young brides.

My *menu du jour* was the Relais de Pantagruel's sole concession to providing food that anyone might actually want to eat, as a break from the vertiginous complexities of the chef's invention; I remember spotting one dish of baked rabbit stuffed with veal tongue in a sauce of crayfish, chocolate, and mandarin oranges, named of course after the chef's daughter (*lapin à la mode de Sylvie*). The Relais had the air of defeated, craven defiance that hangs around struggling restaurants, an atmosphere of optimism coexisting with sliding morale, and the kind words of the customer (in response to the restaurateur's desperate query "Was everything all right?," never more pitiful than when sincere) telling one story while the till receipts and the line of dust on the door lintel tell another. All unsuccessful small businesses are to some extent alike. The air of gloom, of missed opportunity and miscarried ingenuity—"the gap in the market turned out to be a crevasse," as my father put it about a friend who knew something, but as it happened not enough, about rare books—is common to all failing small businesses, whether it be this restaurant (where the standard of cooking wasn't, it turned out, at all bad, the *rillettes* agreeably fatty and the prunes convincingly plump-but-shriveled, like scrotums; the salad refreshing, harlequinesque in hue but not in savor, avoiding the obvious pitfall of being too "interesting" for its own good; the dry bony pike beautifully complemented by the authoritative, shallot-celebrating *beurre blanc;* the *tarte à la crème* light in its pastry but potently calorific in the daffodil-yellow topping), or the dry cleaners in the high street of Wooton in Norfolk, with its too loud entry bell, its motionless crone and gum-chewing teenager watching television behind the Formica counter, the plastic-wrapped clothes on the rail somehow reminiscent of Vietnam War bodybags. My brother once had an atelier above the offices of a veterinarian in Lambeth who had a richly merited reputation for killing his patients—"the taxidermist's friend," Bartholomew used to call him—and the generic typology of failure was present there, too, taking the psychic form of the miasma common to premises, enterprises, and people on the way down, and the physical manifestation of a violently assaulting odor of formaldehyde.

Incidentally, the restaurant was not without a house cocktail of its own: a rustic mixture of red Sancerre and *crème de mûre*. I followed this with a small carafe of acceptable house rosé, a pinot noir with a welcome touch of backbone and a strawberryish attack.

The dining room, in preposterous contrast to the local geography and the mundane stuccoed exterior, was decorated in what the decorator probably called a hunting lodge motif: oak paneling, and a threateningly huge fireplace of the sort in front of which marshmallows were toasted and small boys were tortured in the bad old good old days of the English public school; above it were a ferocious stuffed pike the size of a halibut, an elk's head, and—an Anglophile touch, this—a stuffed fox, with that disquieting air of intelligence they have. There was an arsenal of wall-mounted weapons—a stock big enough to fight a prolonged siege in the event, say, of an un-*communautaire* reinvasion of France by the English; a period photograph of some men in capes and hats standing complacently in front of a small pile of dead wild boar; an execrable painting of a man in a sola topi shooting a tiger at fictionally close range while three wailing native bearers fled, loincloths aflutter; not to mention the great-bearded head and formidable shoulders of—and this was unsentimental even by French standards—a European bison. The dining tables were, to use a much overused and misused word, massive, and the napery so heavily starched that it felt as if it might, if tapped at the correct angle with a sufficiently cunning implement, shatter into fragments. Over the cheese trolley, a stag's antlers defunctly loomed.

The chef emerged from the kitchen as I was enjoying my complimentary second cup of coffee: black as the devil, hot as hell, sweet as sin, this last thanks to a couple of well-judged dabs from the dispenser of low-calorie sweetener, the quality of which has so much improved in the last few years—it used to have a thin, chemical taste that was not at all difficult to reconcile with the statement that, as food labels in the United States so bluntly assert, "this product causes cancer in laboratory animals." One has to guard one's figure as the years roll by. Not that my brother bothered to do so, acquiring toward the end of his life, notwithstanding the upper-body exertions inescapable in the sculptor's craft, what my collaborator referred to as "a gut." As *M. le chef* approached I popped into my mouth the tiny florin-sized lemon tart that had been included in the petits fours, as if in reward for eating everything else (though one high-level criticism might be that the pastry-and-curd combination mimicked too closely, or quoted too narrowly, or created an unfortunate assonance with, the curd-and-pastry combination of the *tarte à la crème*).

The chef's whites were immaculate, his manners formal.

"Was everything to monsieur's liking?"

As I have already implied, the repertoire of permissible responses to this gambit is not large. I made one of them.

I am and have always been good at that kind of thing, my
natural force of personality winning through the shyness
and diffidence of the scholar-artist to make what I feel I
am not flattering myself in thinking is a profound impact
on those ordinary people it is my lot to meet—police offi-
cers to ask directions, or the workmen with whom one
exchanges salutations when one passes them in the streets
of the capital, engaged as they tend to be in reexcavating
the same stretch of street that they were digging up only
a few weeks before. Dante, were he alive today, would
incorporate this regular feature of contemporary urban
life into his revised *Inferno,* with both the street's inhabitants and the workmen trapped in a permanent cycle of
drilling, filling in, and redrilling; though I wonder what
would be an appropriate crime for those so punished to
have committed? Certainly, the modern world's wicked-
nesses—drearily mendacious governments, mediocre
financial crimes, and loathsomely predictable murders, all
of them motivated by either love (hate, jealousy) or
money—can seem less impressive than those known to
Dante himself.

My brother made a set of sculptures on themes from
Dante—inchoate figures emerging from the rock like the
first life-forms clambering out of the primeval ooze, their
struggle to emerge expressive of creative struggle and
obscurely painful to look at, without just being boringly
allegorical of the artist's labors. The sculpture of Ugolino,
a huge stone looming over a smaller boulder, twisted, battered, blasted out, switches between being a depiction of

the relevant incident (literature's most persuasively off-putting portrait of cannibalism) and an abstract composition: sometimes one seems to see one, sometimes the other, as in those visual paradoxes designed to create doubt as to whether one is looking at a vase or two lovers kissing, a pretty butterfly or a wounded polar bear. These sculptures, made in response to a commission by a Norwegian magnate who had invented a kind of hydraulic lever and then cleaned up in shipping, were unfinished at the time of my brother's death. Incompletion is always, in an artistic context, poignant, and the sculptures—whose incompletion also laid an extra gloss on themselves, as if it were the final testimony to the arduousness of the creative process—attracted an especially high price after Bartholomew's demise (the archetypal "good career move"), the Norwegian being bought out by a Texas museum which was starting to collect contemporary sculpture and needed a big acquisition "to get the ball rolling" (as its director said, over a telephone line with a disconcerting two-second lag, like talking to the moon, which I suppose in a sense was what one was doing; he also described Bartholomew as "having a kind of Frink-Moore-Michelangelo thing").

To demonstrate connoisseurship—a mutually flattering process, indeed verging on an outright "stroke"—I murmured an inquiry as to the precise identity of a cheese, which I took to be a Larzac, a flashy guess as there are several closely approximate cheeses. My surmise was correct.

"Is monsieur touring?"

Monsieur indicated that this was so. I then had to spend a few minutes pretending to listen to the chef's advice and directions before he and I parted with mutual expressions of esteem. And indeed, I *was* touring, and had spent that morning motoring joyously and liberatedly along the banks of the Loire, the traffic scant and deferential (once one cleared the *banlieues* of Lorient), the clouds high and scudding, one's Peugeot gratifyingly responsive. The Loire is the French river for the traveler who is serious about his (and can we momentarily, for the purposes of this account, abandon the tiresome pretense that this pronoun is gender-neutral? Any sentences containing the words "a fighter pilot, if he . . ." or "a great philosopher, if he . . ." are specifically intended to exclude all members of the female sex except where otherwise explicitly indicated. Thank you so much) French rivers. It is the river that possesses the highest degree of quiddity, a quality also possessed by the boringly wide, pompous, slow-moving Rhine, which gives the impression of marching in step with the drumbeat of its own history, and by the self-consciously soulful Danube, which has the aura of a talker who has been complimented once too often on his (!) conversation and now never stops being determinedly and affectedly "charming." In France the Seine has all the advantages of Northernness (a quality underrated by our Gallic frenemy) but it is too fatally interested in Paris—it has a Parisian's attitude, an unexamined and not fully defensible sense of its own centrality; the

Gironde, a superb little river in its way, plays too instrumental a role as the *aelixir vitae* for the vines of Bordeaux—being grateful to it would be as naive, as pagan, as feeling grateful to the sun. No, the Rhône is the only other serious contender for fluvial supremacy—magnificently long, authoritative in the varied magnificence of its landscape, and flowing toward the beautiful, vine-tressed, herb-scented sun-drenched landscape of our Northern dreams, the South. And there of course lies the rub. The trouble with the Rhône is that it is, finally, too *obvious*—it is the sort of river that might be designed by a conscientious tourist board. No, the Loire it is: the river that moves sideways across the country, boldly challenging the psychic cartography which decrees that everything about France is aligned from north to south, in a gradual progression toward smaller degrees of latitude and higher degrees Celsius; the river which is central to French history from the time of *Gallia Comata,* the "long-haired Gaul" conquered by the Romans, through the time of the Plantagenets, to the long heroic centuries of château-building, courtly love, and ducal infighting, giving it a historical density and lived-inness excelling anywhere in the country (rivaling, indeed, the taut palimpsest of the English landscape); not to forget the high skies and broad horizons of its central flood plain, home, from 1516 to 1519 (the last three years of his life), of Leonardo da Vinci, he of the unrealizable designs and inventions and great paintings painted on unstabilized and therefore rapidly deteriorating surfaces, incarnate hero of the principle of incompletion, of failure through excessive talent, and of genius which excels in so many media that it fails to leave a lasting memorial in any specific one (the implied underrating of that smugly smirking overdressed chambermaid in the Louvre is fully deliberate); the brute fact that the Loire is, at more than a thousand kilometers, the longest river in France; it is France's least obvious and therefore most compelling wine river; and the fact that since it is unnavigable—too shallow and treacherous to be a means of transportation—it is beautifully unsullied by any human presence (that being confined to the mercantile hubbub of the parallel canal, running from Roanne to Briare, culminating in a droll visual joke where Alexandre Gustave Eiffel's pretty aqueduct carries the canal over the river itself): and therefore the Loire is a mirror or metaphor of the human psyche—treacherous, unnavigable, resistant to banal ideas of *use,* its superficial calm masking uncovenanted depths, hidden velocities. I was certainly looking forward to my afternoon's drive. As I had specified over the telephone, the Peugeot 306 had a glazed sunroof.

The attentive reader may have noticed, in the foregoing, a certain note of relaxation: the leisurely feat of motoring serenely planned in calm anticipation of an uninterrupted agenda; the gazetteer and guidebook relied upon with burgherly confidence; the absence of any other parties, particularly honeymooners, in the restaurant where I had lunched; the telltale apéritif, the giveaway carafe of rosé, the revealing (though, now I think back, I notice not actually revealed—sly me!) *marc de bourgeuil* (a trifle thin and aluminumy in its top notes) helping those two cups of uncompromising espresso on their way, the practice of consuming brandy and coffee at the same time being one of those instances in which human beings consume poison and antidote together. I might mention that in the absence of any disguise the cool air circulating around my recently shaven head was distinctly refreshing.

Nothing of importance can be accomplished without planning. (There is no such thing as a pleasant surprise.) That morning, after checking my honeymooners' whereabouts via a bit of judicious electronic eavesdropping, I had risen at an hour at which my only conscious companions would have been monks arising to sing their predawn orisons, stretching their limbs as they creaked and tottered to the frosty chapel, their breath hanging in the air like *pneuma* or spirit made visible as they chanted, an effort captured in that much recast bronze of my brother's, *The Missal,* a hunched but somehow victorious figure, as exhaustingly overfamiliar as that work of Rodin's my brother used to refer to as *The Snog*—indeed, he would refer to this piece of his own, celebrated for its atmosphere of secular reverence and respect for the idea of worship (one critic remarking that it was "one of agnostic modernity's most forceful and rueful compliments to belief"), as "egg and chips." At that hour in the small Lorient hotel, nothing stirred as I crept, cat-burglarishly silent in a polo sweater and black plimsolls, down the corridor, down the stairs, and across the desk area to the side door which was openable from the inside and was not alarmed, monsieur having confided to the Swiss desk clerk, a graduate of hotel school clearly eager to move on to bigger things, that he was prone to insomnia and wont to take a calming stroll in the small hours. Monsieur was assured that there would not be any problem. And so monsieur went out into the courtyard, where the air had a certain nocturnal crispness, and over which a solitary unshielded bulb presided, burning high up on the becreepered brickwork above the green-painted wooden doors which constituted the yard's outside wall on the rue Thiers.

Their car was, in accordance with the law of maximum inconvenience, usually described as Sod's when it could more accurately be called God's, parked in the middle of the square. As I moved toward it, my body turned sideways to inch between a seven-series BMW with a burglar alarm winking redly in its dashboard and a stodgy old white Volvo with tartan-covered seats, one sweeping glance upward confirming that all the windows on the courtyard were shuttered or curtained (O blessed naked bulb!), I became aware of an animate presence. I froze momentarily before the sense data I had registered just below the threshold of full consciousness coalesced into the form of a large hairy dog, lying in the puddle of yellow light under the thrice-accursed light source, its eyes open and looking straight at me in wary canine alertness—obviously this was a dog that had rudely accosted hotel guests in the past and had learned the hard way the importance of minding its manners. Each of Fido's huge nostrils emitted a small parcel of steam with every stifled pant. Clearly, this could go either way. The dog was a *briard* or *berger de Brie,* I now saw, a shaggy amiable loyal breed, originally used for shepherding and wolf-warding in the Haute-Savoie, its size such that it is almost mistakable for a small pony; the *briard*'s only weakness as a family pet is its well-known tendency to the opposite of longevity. (Etienne's family had had one called Lucille, whose picture he always carried in his wallet along with his bee-sting antidote.) I was, however, emboldened by the fact that in my confrontation with the hound I had, thanks to the tip-off I had planted about my fictional insomnia, the advantage of an impeccably planned alibi, equivalent to a criminal's being able to show that he was onstage at the London Palladium in front of thirteen hundred spectators at the time the crime can be proved to have been committed (slow-acting poison, idle pathologist, doctored clock). Still, the courtyard was much ringed about by, and much overlooked by, windows, and would prove an excellent amphitheater for my potentially scheme-wrecking embarrassment. I therefore put the greatest possible confidence and warmth into my theatrically projected whisper as I lent forward and down, extended a hand palm outward, and urgently hissed:

"Good doggie."

Which did the trick. The beast raised itself to its full Baskervillian height and moved toward me, tail furrily thrashing the air as it padded over the cobbles, a length of rope paying out behind it to a wall-mounted iron stanchion. My canine companion sniffed and licked my left hand while I kept my shoe box–sized package of goodies securely wedged under my right arm—in fact with dog, electronic equipment, and me, it was quite a squeeze in there among the foreign cars. After a few dozen seconds of interspecies fraternization I pushed on with a valedictory "down boy" past my new friend, who turned and followed with a strangely human mixture of curiosity and abject devotion. I slipped nimbly onto my back beside the toy-like but speedy left-hand-drive hired Fiat. Without needing my pencil torch, proceeding by touch, I located the spot recommended by the memorized instructions, flicked back the plastic lid which covered the automatically activated and very powerful electronic magnet on the base of the gadget, and affixed the surprisingly small device—two kitchen-size matchboxes on top of each other, say—to the underside of the wheel well, where any deeply unlikely random inspection (for what? bombs?) would be hard-pressed to descry it, and where the clumsy hands of a mechanic would have no reason to pry.

Back in my room—the noisily whimpering parting with Régine, as a glance at the silvery dog-tag had shown my canine co-conspirator to be properly called, having given me a *mauvais quart de minute* at the end of my expedition—I performed an action which I now, standing beside the Peugeot in the car park at the Relais de Pantagruel, found myself performing again. From my suitcase, tidily stowed in the vehicle's hatchback, I took out a metal box, as oddly heavy as if its internal workings were made of lead or gold, about the size of the boxed Pléiades set of *A la recherche du temps perdu* (the three-volume edition of 1954, with the silly foreword by André Maurois, rather than the portentous, overannotated and illogically divided four-volume edition of 1987). Out of the top of this emerged an aerial, which one extracted by taking a grip of the friendly rubber bobble atop it and pulling out the segmented metal antenna to its full length, about eight inches. ("What's the difference between six and nine inches?" I once witnessed Bartholomew appall a roomful of listeners by asking. "Much Ado About Nothing and Midsummer Night's Dream.") The front edge of the box, beside the aerial, had a rocker switch in a recessed indentation designed to prevent its accidental manipulation— one of those enigmatic switches with a line on one side and a circle on the other, an entirely arbitrary pair of hieroglyphics which never fails to leave one in the dark as to whether the device in question is on or off. The top of the box was an oval dark green laminated plastic screen with a white grid system painted over it. Tiny scratches and imperfections were already starting to mar the device's surface. When I turned on the rocker the machine performed various contented whinings ("self-test," the helpful salesman had explained to my unspoken query) before projecting a single light green dot more or less exactly in the middle of the central grid.

"Obviously this doesn't tell you everything you need to know on its ownsome," said the salesman, a short man whose kemptness and grooming were in strange contrast with the riotous profusion of hardware and ironmongery in his shop—screws, ratchets, spanners of a size to adjust everything from the watches in a doll's house to a life-sized mechanical elephant, Swiss Army knives, inflatable ducks, daggers and nunchatkas, arrow targets, crossbows. The only aspects of his demeanor which echoed the some-how intentful crowdedness of his shop's decor were his propelled manner of speaking and the two leaping upthrusts of hair that sprang from his ears like grass on a cliff ledge. I had found the shop in the classified section of a magazine specializing in weapons, with an interesting sideline in the paraphernalia of surveillance and industrial espionage.

Not that the small gray box on its own constituted adequate technological backup. The little man in the shop (paradigmatically useful in the sense that "little men," invariably manual laborers with a satisfying air of knowing their place, always are—it's one of my favorite pieces of patronizing English middle-class speech) had been firm on this point, and we had spent an important twenty minutes or so on the principles and practice of using a compass, gridding and taking reckonings from a remarkably phallic building visible downriver toward the East End.

"The RDF on its own won't get you all the way," the shopkeeper had explained. "You need a compass to track down what direction your bloke's heading in and a map to work out what that means. Also the grid won't tell you exactly where he is once you're in the immediate vicinity. Under a hundred yards or so. But that's not generally a problem. As a general rule if you've got your map, your compass, and your RDF, you've got your geezer."

I stocked up on maps later that same afternoon at a specialist retailer in Covent Garden. The helpful assistant, who had an unblemished café au lait complexion and permanently surprised eyebrows, had shown me the section of the shop specializing in France, a more compendious collection than it at first appeared to be, since the waist-level display of goods concealed below it several further drawers, which could be pulled out and inspected like the exhibit cases in nineteenth-century science museums. There is an especially extensive range of such cases in the Pitt-Rivers Museum, where my brother used to spend the two hours a day the premises were open when he was researching a design for a totem pole—a commission from the Duke of Rothborough, who had just discovered that thanks to some antics by his vastly more adventurous great-great-grandfather he was, technically speaking, the tribal chieftain of a group of Huron Indians in southeastern Canada, or at least he could have been if the Indians hadn't all been killed by colds and smallpox. (History gives us every reason to suppose that these diseases were transmitted to the Hurons—who, incidentally, don't make totem poles—by the very same ancestor.) The pole depicts the family animal, a stag. It still stands in front of the Rothboroughs' ancestral home in Lincolnshire, and very peculiar it looks, too.

The selection of maps was so large that it was on the thin margin between enticing and daunting. I contemplated for a moment the purchase of a book, the Michelin 1:200000 being the obvious front-runner, before settling for a series of adjacent maps of the same scale, covering the whole of the country, my logic being that although self-contained paper maps are at a disadvantage in windy conditions, the smallest gust of air turning a routine exercise in navigation into something resembling a life and death struggle between a snorkeler and a manta ray, at least they lack the crucial weakness of constantly forcing one to turn the pages and recalibrate one's bearings in the process.

Naturally, I took pains to develop the skills necessary for the successful use of my sexy new gadget. Standing in the aftermath of lunch at the Relais de Pantagruel, I repeated a procedure that I had practiced "for real" from the cottage in Norfolk, in a vertiginously overexciting morning spent dashing around country lanes in pursuit of my target. My object then was Ron the milkman and his van. I had lain in wait across the road, hiding behind the beech tree that grows outside the Wilsons' much-burgled holiday cottage, then sneaking up on the blind side of the whining vehicle and sticking my electronic marvel to the underside of the chassis while Ron walked up the path and switched a spick new pint of silver-top for the conscientiously washed empty one I had left out for him, as per my Friday routine. I then strolled oh-so-casually past the returning milk board functionary in his white coat—Morning, Ron!—before closing the door, counting to one hundred, and scurrying back outside to vault into my unlocked Audi. And then a stimulating morning pottering around the countryside, making mistakes and learning from them, each of the chief lessons having attached to it the error which precipitated its formulation. 1) Always stop to check the map, don't try to calibrate bearings on the hoof: I had nearly driven into the back of a Transit-van-cum-ambulance full of pensioners outside Fakenham. 2) Confidence about the object's general whereabouts is more important than minute certainty as to his exact location: I had got stuck behind a tractor with manure-encrusted wheels while trying to stay too close to Ron's tail, had panicked, and had then overtaken, very inappropriately, over a blind humpbacked bridge, flashing as I did so past the whitely startled face of a lucky bicyclist. 3) Be aware that once you get close to the object, extreme care is needed: I had walked around a corner and straight into Ron at the end of his rounds in the council estates, and only great presence of mind had allowed me to blurt out a plausible excuse for the morning's second apparently chance encounter. "Just checking on the marrow!" I cried, relying on the probability that Ron would know the whereabouts of the council allotments, and would not be too troubled by either the fact that I was not dressed for gardening, or that I had a garden of my own anyway. Ten minutes later, when he had parked outside the Pig and Whistle (celebrated for its rice puddings, and a valuable customer of the local milk board) and trudged 'round the back to effect his large scale drop-off and collect, I double-parked, left the engine running, and claimed back my vindicated transmitter, in the process learning lesson 4), i.e., it's stuck on more firmly than you think, and the spring-release clip is hard to find when reaching blindly with the fingertips, a gesture oddly like the one involved in pushing my mother's earrings under Mary-Theresa's mattress. In Fakenham I had a nasty moment of real crisis, time simultaneously expanding and contracting as I fumbled to spring the tiny clip, and had barely got away, Ron appearing from the back of the pub in the rearview mirror as I hotly cornered.

Thus practiced, I stood in the restaurant car park at the end of the long cypress-lined drive, smoothly tarmacked to compel the attention of the Michelin inspectors, their descent as chargedly anonymous as that of an angel in a legend. I took the map out and (good trick) spread it on the still warm bonnet of the Peugeot, holding each of its corners in place with a firm dab of reusable adhesive putty. Calculating with the compass, the Range and Direction Finder, and the map, its colors brighter and its symbols less useful than those of the trusty ordnance survey 1:10000 jobs on which I had cut my teeth, I obtained a result which I can safely say, without being smug, failed to surprise me. Near Loudun there is a small forest which some well-meaning art lovers commissioned my brother to turn into a "sculpture park."

A Selection of
Cold Cuts

The Russian *zakuski,* Polish *zakaski,* Greek *meze,* Rumanian *mezeliuri,* German *Abendbrot,* French *hors d'oeuvre,* and classic English cold table—these come into their own when divorced from their original cultural contexts (which, in the case of the East European variants, tends to be to do with helping down battleship-floating quantities of alcohol) and translated into the international lingua franca of summer cooking. There can be no better way of physically experiencing the length of days than to assemble a *saucisson* here, a *salade de tomates* there, a cucumber *raita* and slice of *pissaladière,* some boiled eggs, a portion of *ratatouille,* some olives, anchovies, a local cheese or two, raw fresh baby turnips, smoked fish, smoked roe, *pro-sciutto,* marinated aubergines, hummus, mushrooms or leeks *à la grecque,* and such pâtés and terrines as judicious experiments with local suppliers will provide, perhaps a cold roast bird to fiddle with, the whole accompanied by good butter and good bread and washed down by an ideally unpretentious local wine. One's digestion responds to the warmth and promised indolence of summer by seeming to slow down, to reject the Annapurnas and K2s, the challenges represented by the more substantial fare of winter; one feels the need to pick and choose, to intrigue the palate with a variety of treats and excellences rather than to confront the appetite head-on, as in a gladiatorial contest between the *retiarius* and the *murmillo,* the net-swinger with the cruel trident and the heavily armored myrmidon—this having been the clash that especially excited my youthful imagination, much more so than the boringly one-sided encounter between lions and Christians (a form of public execution which I notice fails to be mentioned by penal theorists discussing the rival merits of lethal injection versus firing squad versus electric chair). Who can resist the eudaemonic combination of meteorology and gastronomy represented by a cold lunch on a hot day? Who can begrudge a young couple on honeymoon a simple picnic in the park, strolling among the works of nature and the deeds of man, hand in hand, in the afternoon, in the Loire, in love?

It was at a time when my brother's work had taken on a more abstract, celebratory, and pantheistic tenor that he embarked on the sculpture-park project. I remember teasing him about the venture one day in his East London fastness, over the debris of a take-away "Indian" that his then mistress had collected from their preferred local curry house, in the process incomprehensibly substituting a lamb *vindaloo* for the lamb *dhansak* I had in fact ordered. As I observed at the time, " 'vindaloo' does not sound very like 'dhansak' even if the person being spoken to is exceptionally stupid."

"Your precipitate social decline cannot fail to alarm your well-wishers," I told my brother. "You started as a painter, then you became a sculptor, now you're basically a sort of gardener. What next, Barry? Street cleaner? Lavatory attendant? Journalism?"

"Perhaps I am getting soft," Bartholomew admitted. "I'm more interested than I used to be in beauty and less interested in force. Force of the imagination, tour de force. Water, stone, trees, sunlight. Pass the chutney."

"Pig," said Alice (Alex? Alicia?), who had her moments.

In the fullness of time, I went to the opening of the park, which was, this being France, preceded by an alfresco lunch in a central forest glade, the weather having narrowly "held." Various art-world notables and a collection of local dignitaries were feasted by the sponsors of the project. The menu was judiciously untesting—lark pâté, lamb cutlets, *bourdaines* (apples stuffed with jam made out of a local peach-apricot hybrid called *alberge de Tours*). I was in the area partly to sneer at Bartholomew's project and partly to investigate the local delicacies of the Saumur region, especially the *andouillette* made out of eel and horse tripe—*andouillette* being my favorite offal, firmly regarded as inedible by my brother, who had decided that it was "too smelly." Whereas, of course, the smelliness is part of the point—less the literal odor than the thrilling sense of taint, the bawareness one encounters in the act of eating offal, more than at any other time, that one is eating, putting inside one's stomach, the flesh of a dead fellow-animal.

A rich Bavarian in a silk suit with a dark gray weave made a speech which consisted of lightly coded boasting about his own wealth, generosity, and foresight as a patron of the arts, combined with various implausible claims about my brother's work. A female French art critic with (the most cursory of previous encounters had established) truly *astonishing* halitosis stood porkily up and talked nonsense about Bartholomew's "oscillation between *sprezzatura* and *terribilità.*" The mayor of Chinon, who did not seem overprepared for the occasion, made a plea for reelection. And then the tour of the park began, the assembled worthies being allowed to disperse and wander around at will. Some of them, having lunched not wisely but too well, seized the opportunity to head off for a quiet spot and seek a fortifying snooze. And of course, there turned out to be something of a scandal about *le parc qui n'existe pas,* as one of the dailies had it—the point of my brother's project being the integration of small stone works into the ordinary landscape of the forest so that they failed to make an impact as conscious "works of art" at all—a stone here, a cairn there, a bench or a picnic table elsewhere. The effect has been described as Japanese, ironically, given Bartholomew's oft-expressed earlier commitment to the belief that "less is less." (Bartholomew hardly ever expressed thoughts or opinions on the larger issues of aesthetics, which is probably just as well, since when he did so it was always in a spirit comparable to that which Flaubert described in himself when the talk turned to literary topics and he felt like a former convict listening to a conversation about prison reform. Bartholomew was comparably gruff, irritably concrete, dismissively well-informed and insiderly in a way that it would have been possible intensely to resent. "Most of what people say about art is bollocks," he once said to me, in the aftermath of some television program about his work—I myself not possessing a set had viewed the documentary in the presence of its subject at his studio premises in Leytonstone, the ultrafashionably unfashionable area where he worked and where he therefore, as an adjunct or afterthought, in a gesture as marginal as the act of signing a painting, lived. "There are only three questions asked in art: Who am I? And who are you? And what the fuck's going on?")

I would not be visiting the park that day. I was planning to do nothing more than potter about. My afternoon itinerary was going to consist of a long-contemplated visit to Seuilly, where there is a pompous château, a street of charming cave houses, and a few miles outside, the birthplace of François Rabelais, one of literature's great putter-inners. (My collaborator, pressed by me to provide a definition or distinction between modernism and post-modernism—she having used the latter term to make some low-level though well-intentioned point about what kind of artist my brother wasn't—said that "Modernism is about finding out how much you could get away with leaving out. Post-modernism is about how much you can get away with putting in.") I was hoping also that there would be time to drop in on Fontevraud Abbey. The abbey was a favorite of the Plantagenets, who built it up into the considerable agglomeration of buildings (five in all) which it is today—the last resting place of King Henry II, his wife Eleanor, and their swashbuckling son Richard Coeur de Lion. Fontevraud also houses the hearts of King John, that bad egg to whom we owe the existence of the Magna Carta, and of goody-goody Henry III, his unlikely son; though the news that someone's body has been buried in one place, his heart in another, always brings to my mind not the noble idea of a hard-earned rest from labor, but the image of a gruesome postmortem evisceration. (What, for instance, do they carry the heart in? Who cuts it out?) The Plantagenets have always been my favorite of the English royal dynasties, less oafish than all those dreary Anglo-Saxon warrior chieftains who preceded them, less fratricidal than the Yorkists and Lancastrians, less untrustworthy and megalomaniacal than the unforgivably Welsh Tudors, less silly than the Stuarts, and less German than everybody since, the house of Saxe-Coburg-Gotha most emphatically not excepted. Eleanor must have been quite a handful—thrice-kidnapped before marriage by besotted suitors, the first of whom was A) her future husband's brother and B) twelve years younger than she; she spent the latter half of her life inciting her sons, John Lackland and Richard Coeur de Lion, against their father. I've always thought of her as being a little like my mother, except with a higher IQ and a longer attention span. Eleanor was divorced—the divorced wife of the French king—and brought with her as her dowry the lands of Poitou, the Saintorge, Limousin, and Gascony, which puts into perspective the modest estate I inherited on the death of my parents.

Before that, though, I paid a brief visit to Chinon, the home of one of my favorite wines, made out of the tangy, expressive, stalky Cabernet Franc, capable of seeming both playful and fruity in some moods, darker and even a touch forbidding in others, though without ever really preparing to challenge the peaks or plumb the abysses (of sensation, of expectation) which grander and more ambitious wines inhabit as their landscape—a wine like a lake, say, changing moods widely according to the play of light across wind and chopping wavelets, and capable of annually drowning a fisherman or two, while never straying from its determining scale of lakeness.

I arrived in the early mid-afternoon and mooched briefly around the slope of the great old castle where Henry II had died; funny to think that from this spot he ruled a kingdom stretching from the foothills of the Pyrenees to the grouse-infested moors of the Scottish borders.

Again, England would then have been a significantly more livable-in country than it is today—with a sweaty, uncouth, but hardworking and properly subjugated Anglo-Saxon peasantry securely in its place, and a Norman nobility making the transition from opportunistic plunderers in longboats to tapestry-commissioning, French-speaking castle dwellers, an early but very spectacular form of social climbing and self-improvement. (The bulk of the country, covered with thick forests, would have yielded a plentiful supply of wild mushrooms, venison, and wild boar, the latter especially tasty when it is allowed a copious diet of its favorite food, the acorn.) Chinon, however, is now nothing more than a memory of itself, thanks to its Pyrrhic convenience as a stopping-off point for tourists to the Loire as much as to its intrinsic interest. There was a brief but irritating traffic jam on the way out of town, where a school bus decanting its vociferous contents (the French holding the European palm for noisiest schoolchildren) had got into an impasse (literally) with two German camper vans. The ensuing standoff offered a fatally easy and boring metaphor of European history between 1870 and 1945.

Just outside Chinon I spotted a turnoff for a château I had never heard of before, the Château d'Herbault, and impulsively lurched off the main road to give the place a hypercritical and well-informed once-over. My car and I purred up the crunchy driveway toward a boxy-looking seventeenth-century structure with unusually small windows. I wondered momentarily, before banishing the thought from my consciousness like a monarch exiling a felon or a samurai warrior beheading a peasant simply to test the sharpness of his sword—I wondered what my young friends had bought for lunch and where they bought it, whether they had taken advice about what charcuterie-pâtisserie-boulangerie-épicerie to visit, or had merely opted for pot luck. My brother, when he was most fully engaged on a work project, would cease to eat properly constituted meals, as if he were taking Auden's advice—"The artist is living in a state of siege"—too literally to heart, and were snatching his opportunities to eat in the rare intervals between kicking enemy climbing frames away from the walls, extinguishing fire-arrow conflagrations, and pouring boiling oil onto the attackers' heads. Bartholomew would dignify his habits by referring to them as "picnicking"—which in practice involved eating whole loaves of bread while pacing around the studio, accompanying this with whole packets of processed cheese, half-jars of pickles, cold sausages, sliced ham, and baked beans eaten straight out of the tin while standing up and marching about like a Scotsman at his porridge. I once thoughtfully dropped in to check up on his well-being when he was engaged on finishing a piece of work—an allegorical Heracles, writhing in an allegorial shirt of Nessus that on closer inspection turned out to be the hide of an animal—taking with me a small but well-thought-out hamper of the piquant foods and condiments he most enjoyed (he was "between girlfriends"), only to have him announce "Great—I'm starving," before eating an entire jar of French gherkins and falling asleep on his disreputable coffee-colored sofa. While finishing the sculpture park in the *forêt de l'Aude,* he made a lasting impact on the local workmen by appearing to subsist on nothing except red Sancerre and chocolate digestive biscuits—a delicacy with which they were hitherto unacquainted, but with whose fortificatory properties they declared themselves *"vraiment impressionnés."*

It was pleasant, very pleasant, to be able to forgo the clothes and wigs that had been my constant companions for the last few days, and were now crumpled ignored in two capacious suitcases in the Peugeot's boot. With the vehicle's sunroof rolled back, my head was exposed to the elements in the most soothing manner imaginable, currents of air circulating around it like tradewinds around the earth herself. I should explain that the succession of muftis and incogniti with which I have so far graced this narrative is not my conventional, or perhaps habitual would be a better word, attire. My shaven head, for instance, despite being such a practical and easily maintained way of wearing one's hair, has been known to affect some people as being at odds with other items of my wardrobe, perhaps especially my collection of suits, such as the large-patterned check suit, my favorite, which I was wearing that day in tribute to the free time I had been granted by the auspicious conjunction of map, compass, RDF, and my own ingenuity. These green and ochre checks were complemented, or perhaps that should be complimented, by my shirt, a pale cerise cotton number with a fine texture showing—though only at close range and to the discerning eye—a diagonally shading pattern; I also wore a bow tie with yellow polka dots against a light blue background, a matching display handkerchief, a fob-watch and chain, and a superbly conservative pair of handmade brown brogues.

I pulled up into the château car park at about four in the afternoon. There was the usual crush of tourist cars, and a festering coach or two. I resolved not to linger, a correct decision, as the château's contents and history were dull, and the premises were horribly crowded with jostling hordes of *ignorami.* The low-grade provincial squires of the Herbault family seemed never to have done, bought, or thought anything of particular interest. Their château did, however, have a redeeming feature in the form of the family mausoleum, a nicely laid-out room with some not-bad funeral statuary, the last pre-Revolutionary duke having apparently been buried with not one or even two but four (4) of his favorite staghounds. The marble was beautifully cold. Clearly nothing in life became the Herbaults as much as being dead.

It's strange how the mind works. The funeral stone, which should have reminded me of my brother, who did after all work with it (*The Diver,* the Catalan Pietà), instead spoke to me, as it always does, of poor Mitthaug, through a complex association of ideas to do with marble reminding me of snow (color, temperature, purity), and snow reminding me of our Norwegian servant; my youthful imagination having firmly fastened on Norway as a

country in a permanent condition of emblanketed whiteness, the human beings outnumbered by polar bears as
sheep outnumber people in New Zealand. (That was a fact
which had made a powerful impression on me: it brought
to mind the possibility that the sheep might one day *take
over.*) Somehow the appropriateness of marble in a funer-
ary context has to do with the metaphorical connection,
the rhyme, between the coolness of the stone and the chill
of dead human flesh. It is partly, of course, marble's very
perfection that intensifies the association with death—
and like all perfect things, marble is inert. Perhaps that is
why the worker-artists of the Middle Ages, so often
underrated in preference to the self-promoting *précieux* of
the Renaissance, seem to have disliked the stone, preferring more workable and more expressive media, and also
having an enthusiasm for color and variegation one of
whose strengths is that it was not always in good taste.

Mitthaug's death was generally seen as taking place in
that liminal area between accident and suicide. It is a field
which offers extensive opportunities to those who seek to
interpret the motives of others and to know the secrets of
the human heart, to plumb the abysses (my personal view:
no point). The facts: He fell in front of a District Line
train at Parsons Green station; I was with him, though I
explained to the inquest that I wasn't able to be of much
use as a witness, owing to the struggle I had been undergoing with my mittens, which my mother had arranged
to be fastened together with a piece of elastic that was
slightly too short and which required me to pin one mit-

ten to my side with an elbow inside the coat before tugging the second one into place with my hand and forcing my fingers into it. An unstraightforward operation at the best of times, limiting my freedom of movement and taking up a lot of attention. It seems that Mitthaug simply stepped forward and lost his footing at precisely the wrong moment, just as the train was hurtling into the station. I was spared some of the more gruesome details— including presumably the worst one of all as the train, now denuded of passengers, reversed down the track to reveal the dismembered body of our former cook, jointed like a chicken for casseroling—by the fact that a nice fat woman, who had seen Mitthaug and me enter the station together, had straightaway taken me to the nearest policeman she could find. They had a whispered conversation while I ate the gobstopper with which I had been bribed. I was then taken home by a different policeman, who had the first Geordie accent I had ever heard. At Bayswater a sequence of distressing news-breakings took place; only my father had the honest vulgarity to say what everyone was thinking: "Not again." The inquest jury returned an open verdict, though the coroner, otherwise charming (at least to me, then aged twelve, and naturally the star witness), seemed inclined to reach a finding of suicide, not least I think because one of Mitthaug's brothers had apparently also, in my father's words, "bumped himself off." (The coroner rejected out of hand the "evidence" of a plainly hysterical woman who claimed to have seen me administering a well-timed shove to Mitthaug's back just as the train arrived on the platform.) Mitthaug was not known to have money or love troubles and left no note, but his former "weakness for the sherbert," as my father put it, was no secret; he was also a great reader of his own and cognate countrymen's literature (Strindberg, Ibsen) and the coroner seemed to feel that counted for quite a bit. Still, open verdict it was.

There's something about inquests and funerals that never fails to sharpen the appetite. On the day of Mitthaug's inquest my parents took me to Fortnum's for tea; I ate fourteen scones. (A personal best.) Which is why I had moved on to thinking about the relative merits of muffins, scones, and the traditional English cream tea as I emerged from the mausoleum at the Château d'Herbault, following the approved and signposted tourist route, climbing up into the sunlight and the colonnade, turning a corner and coming within about six inches of walking straight into the back of the young couple whom I had, not to put too fine a point on it, been following. To say this was a complete disaster would be a terrible understatement. I was facing a *débâcle.*

"No accident that *débâcle* is a French word," observed my brother once at a hideously mismanaged unveiling ceremony near his home in Arles. In that case, the first set of attempts to unveil a sculpture had gone awry: the twitch on the rope ostentatiously failed to dislodge the monument's elaborate cloth façade, and an overalled mechanic eventually had to cut the figure free. The word *débâcle* suggests the going-wrong of an elaborately conceived plan: a disaster that somehow leaves the principal parties not only having lost what they were aware that they were risking but much more besides, as if an attempt to charm the boss by inviting him to dinner and cooking an ambitious favorite dish of his were to result in the death by poisoning of his wife, the loss of one's job, collapse of one's marriage, one's bankruptcy, turn to violent crime, and subsequent death in a shoot-out with police—when all one was worried about was the risk of curdling the hollandaise. Compare the implication of mismanagement, of organization going wrong, in the Gallic *débâcle* with the candidly chaotic, intimate quality of the Italian *fiasco,* or the blokishly masculine and pragmatic (and I would suggest implicitly reversible and therefore, in its deep assumptions, optimistic) American *fuck-up.* As I have already remarked, I had festively, and, I now saw, recklessly, shed all disguise, and my clothing is not undistinctive. The sole cause for anything other than panic was the fact that my presence was as yet, thanks to a distracting collision between two electric wheelchairs about thirty yards ahead, undetected. The encounter was turning into a gesticulatory argument; for a moment it seemed as if a form of jousting might be about to take place.

I shuffled backward behind the pillar around which moments before I had so heedlessly careened. But how was I to make my escape? My couple's perspective was such that I was standing in the only point of the colonnade unsurveilled by them, in the dogleg immediately to their rear. But any advance toward the exit would bring me into their full view, while retreating into the crypt through the door marked *"sortie interdite"* would be unthinkable, not least because the door had no handle. For a moment I deliriously contemplated climbing into the suit of armor standing against the wall and making a lumbering, clanking dash for it. Or perhaps a better strategy would be to hide in the armor until nightfall and then to tell the guards that I had fallen asleep in the lavatory. But no—I must keep calm. In this context the French formulation of that injunction, to be found on instructions about fire, airplane crashes, and sinking ferries, is helpful: *Gardez votre sang-froid.* It was highly unlikely that I would be able to make my way around the cloister unseen, and any moment now a chance movement on their part might bring me into full view, as magnificent, as solitary, and as unmistakable as an elk in a telescopic rifle-sight.

I have always been fond of Sherlock Holmes's axiom to the effect that once the improbable has been ruled out, the solution must lie in the realm of the impossible. As I stood in the corner of the enclosure, my back pressed against the heavy doors of the mausoleum, I suddenly remembered my brother's maxim that "no exit" always means "exit." So I stood my ground, the young couple now heaving into sight in front of me, and then, as a Japanese tour party, led by a guide in a mackintosh carrying a folded orange umbrella, emerged from the interior, I skillfully caught the door back into the crypt with my toe and held it wedged open while the forty or so culture lovers emerged before losing patience, swaying around the last few of them, and barging back into the crypt against the flow of traffic, passing the objects and memorials of the Château d'Herbault at speed and in reverse— like watching a film being rewound. *"C'est interdit!"* cried a guard as I shouldered my way powerfully out of the entrance, the certainty of my fortunate escape upwelling within me as I scuttled across the car park, bounded into my Peugeot, and roared off toward Fontevraud. Though even at the time I was interested to notice that the guard could instinctively identify me as being fluent in French.

· *Autumn* ·

An *Aïoli*

A Breakfast

A Barbecue

An Omelette

An *Aïoli*

It is not really an exaggeration to say that peace and happiness begin, geographically, where garlic is used in cooking." Thus X. Marcel Boulestin, a hero of Anglo-French culinary interaction inexplicably omitted from *Larousse Gastronomique.* And which of us has not felt the truth of Boulestin's words as we arrive in that land whose very name seems to betoken and evoke a widening of life's sensuous possibilities, the addition of an extra few notes at either end of one's emotional keyboard, a set of new stops on the church organ of the psyche, an expansion of every cell of one's sensory paraphernalia, a new rapprochement between body, mind, and spirit; that land which is also an idea, a medium, a métier, a program, an education, a philosophy, a cuisine, a word: Provence. (On rereading that sentence I discover that, grammatically, it requires a question mark which I am, however, reluctant to supply.) Who ever forgets his (!) first arrival in this enchanted region, motoring south, either sprinting down the *autoroute* or weaving down through the Massif Central, before finding that subtle, and then increasingly less so, alteration in climate and topography which denotes—or is it connotes?—The South. I myself undertook such a journey in the days immediately preceding the events I am about to describe (outside table at a café under a lime tree in L'Isle-sur-la-Sorgue; *citron pressé;* noise of the Sorgue pouring under nearby footbridge; mopeds; 11 A.M.).

And this of course is an essentially comic notion, notwithstanding Alfred Jarry's perception that clichés are the armature of the absolute. The encounter between the North and the South has been one of Europe's defining, organizing misprisions, one whose forms have the continuity-in-mutability of identities in a dream: the strange meeting of cultured Visigoth, with his ability to quote Catullus and his interest in architecture, and brutish Roman; the Viking working as a guard in the palace forecourts of Byzantium or—in that wonderful Viking word for that most wonderfully named of cities—Miklagard; the Normans in Sicily; the labored misapprehensions of British travelers on the grand tour, frightened of brigands and thunderstorms; Goethe self-intoxicatedly fornicating in Rome; Byron and his countesses and his politics; coach parties at the papal palace in Avignon. The Northern travelers who have had a genuine understanding of the mind of the South are few and if I count myself in their number it is not so much because of anything that I have done as because of my instinctive understanding of the rhythms and imperatives of life in the *mezzogiorno*—life within the earshot of cicadas. To put it another way, there are few people born within a culture that does not use olive oil as its primary cooking medium who can claim a genuine liking for *pastis* and its associated alcohols.

I had sat at this same café on my first evening in Provence as a local householder—a pleasantly "undiscovered" local joint, serving a perfectly decent *croque-monsieur* that I in subsequent years was to teach them to enliven with a dab of mustard in the sauce mixture. The laborious negotiations and the elaborate bureaucracy of all French legal transactions had made the whole process a long drawn-out and stressful one, enlivened only by the entertainingly transparent duplicity of the curmudgeonly Belgian couple who were the former freeholders—an early-morning raid on the day preceding that of the purchase caught them in the act of attempting to repatriate a fridge-freezer and washing machine which were expressly included in the terms of sale. They expressed guilt in the way adults often do, in the form of bad temper. I think they thought that I would be made woozy and dupable by grief: "*Ses parents sont morts dans une grande explosion de chaudière,*" my lawyer had said, causing an expression of music-hall cunning to enter the husband's already porcine eyes.

That first evening, I had left the house unlocked and motored through fields of vine and olive to L'Isle-sur-la-Sorgue to sit on the terrace, where I had drunk a sequence of Ricards and reflected on the consummation of my relationship with the Mediterranean. My first visit to the region had been paid for by my parents as an eighteenth-birthday present; I had gone to stay with my brother, then living and working in a cottage outside Arles. We established a routine whereby I would pile onto my bike and head for the boulangerie, épicerie, boucherie, and fish stall before lingering over a tisane in, or more often exhibitionistically outside, one particular stylishly run-down café; in later years I would hurtle precariously into the village on my little mobylette, which didn't always manage to carry me all the way up the hill under its own power; I would return with a rucksack full of baguettes and pâté for immediate consumption, and more substantial fare for later in the day.

Is it clear that I am very much at home here? This, broadly speaking, is where I have spent the intervening week since the events I am about to relate, dividing my time between this café and my own modest house while I typed up these culinary musings and reflections, the day being divided into sections as follows: quick burst into "town" for a café noir, a round of *saluts,* and provisionings; café au lait on the terrace in the morning sunlight; break for simple luncheon (omelette, Vichy, peaches; tomato salad, garlic soup; *terrine de campagne,* ratatouille baguette), also on the patio, before the sun takes full possession of his demesne; afternoon nap in deckchair by poolside ficus tree, set just far enough back to prevent leaves shedding into the water; dip; fortifying cup of Twinings English Breakfast; second dip; trip to café, and then a frugal meal there or at an intelligently unambitious local hostelry.

In culinary terms, the culmination of any Northern relationship with the South is likely to be expressed through an engagement with garlic. This plant (whose Latin name derives from the Celtic word for "hot"; may we surmise that Mary-Theresa's ancestors ate the plant as part of some fog-shrouded Druidic ritual?) has been the subject of controversy and praise since Roman times, feared for its pungency and revered for its quasi-medicinal properties. The people of Northern and Eastern Europe have never been wholehearted consumers of the freely growing bud, whose suggestion of tangy physicality and pleasure is perhaps too much for what W. H. Auden, himself a not uncomic representative of the encounter between South and North, called a "beer-and-potato guilt culture."

For some, though, the thought of cooking without garlic is—well, let it suffice to call it unthinkable (a word which is in itself, incidentally, self-refuting). Garlic's centrality in my own cuisine is not to be dissimulated. This fact is something I like to celebrate, on the occasion of my arrival in France, with a *grand aïoli,* a feast in which garlic plays a central and sacred role: the legendary garlic mayonnaise is served with a selection of

accompaniments arranged around it, and one of the pleasures of the dish is its inversion of the relationship
between bit part (sauce) and star player (as my young
friend puts it, "the protein bit").

This, of course, is one of the secret delights of many of
the world's most popular dishes—the curry sauce which
is no more than an alibi for its basmati rice, the barons of
beef which are simply an official justification for their
Yorkshire pudding (the French sometimes hint at this
relationship in the possessive pronouns of their menu
descriptions—*ris de veau et* sa *petite salade de lentilles de
Puy,* as if there were only one possible companion in the
whole world and their bond were an indecipherably intimate one, like a marriage or a psychic link between
twins). So it's a useful trick to remember when in pursuit
of crowd-pleasing culinary effects: just invert the conventional relationship between component parts of a
meal, for instance allowing a simple piece of grilled meat
to be outshone by an astonishingly accomplished tureen
of mashed potato. (Think of a motorized cavalcade in
which the royal personage, rather than huddling in the
armored and heralded central limousine, instead flashes
past at the head of the motorcycle outriders.) There is a
familiar phenomenon in all fields of artistic endeavor,
whereby overdelicate or portentously pseudo-epic works
in all media can yield unsought moments of truth when
the artist is looking elsewhere (the chapel my brother
built at Dugois in Belgium, purportedly a masterpiece,
is in fact a classic example of this: an overworked and

overstrenuous large-scale conception—pillars writhing monumentally upward etcetera, redeemed by the simplicity and dashed-offness of an architectural element which he clearly neglected to think about and hence to spoil: to wit, the delightfully lighthearted, unmusclebound, and under-purposeful goblet-shaped font, which to this day goes wholly unremarked by critics and guidebooks alike).

Aïoli. This dish is regarded with mystic fervor in my adopted Provençal homeland, and holds a high place in the local folklore for culinary, cultural, and medical reasons. Pierre and Jean-Luc are especial partisans of the sauce, and during the preparation of the *aïoli monstre* which supplies the centerpiece of the village's summer fête (whose other high spot is the septuagenarian *curé*'s fascinatingly bad hand-puppet show) they are to be found moving from house to house anxiously supervising the preparation of the gleaming sauce, the soothing poached *morue,* the garden-crisp boiled vegetables, all of which will later be served in the square before the war memorial, the list of tragic surnames in family clumps *morts pour la patrie* gazing down at the three sides of trestle tables, the sun high and hot, the rosé copious, four generations of St-Eustache present, all elevated in the high dominion of garlic. It is from the brothers that I acquired my own technique for aïoli, with its candid acceptance of the role of the blender in preference to the laboriously authentic hand-mounted mortar-and-pestle aïoli of tradition: put two egg yolks in a blender with four cloves of garlic and slowly whiz in a pint of olive oil (*ail* meaning "garlic" and *oli* being the term for "olive oil" in Provence's attractively rough-and-ready local dialect) and the juice of a lemon. The dish retains its mystique despite the simplicity of its preparation, an interesting refutation of Marx's theory of surplus as well as his account of the fetish.

My brother, who didn't much like what he with self-conscious unpretentiousness called "foreign food" (a category from which he excluded curry), was nonetheless an enthusiast for garlic, especially in the form of the aïoli currently under discussion: "the nearest thing the French have to HP sauce," I remember him saying, as he ladled another dollop of the ambrosial confection onto his plate (this was while he was living in Brittany, close to a bistro which routinely prepared an *aïoli garni* as its Friday lunchtime special). When he visited me at my house in Provence after the death of our parents—my house bought with the proceeds of their estate, when he was still spending summers at his hutch outside Arles—he would always insist on my constructing an aïoli of the classic Provençal marque, with a cold poached piece of fish as the central dish (often, controversially, not salt cod), or a personal selection of boiled meats, and an intelligent array of accompaniments ranged 'round like an edible honor guard (boiled eggs, asparagus spears, broccoli florets, peeled fava beans, carrots, haricots verts, warm new potatoes in their jackets or, as the Italian expression has it, in their nightshirts, tomatoes, celery, beetroot, chickpeas, and a half-pint or so of simmered escargots). Consumed in large quantity, aïoli can have a stifling effect, so any companion dishes should be light and invigorating; I myself prefer to serve only a tossed green salad (with a magnanimously garlic-free vinaigrette) and some fruit. The preferred libation is the local rosé wine. Frédéric Mistral, to the very best of my knowledge the only poet ever to have been named after a major European wind, wrote that "aïoli epitomizes the heat, the power, and the joy of the Provençal sun, but it has another virtue—it drives away flies." In 1891 Mistral founded a literary journal called *L' aïoli.*

It was with the tentative plan of constructing such a dish that I ventured into Apt one morning a few days ago. Apt is a market town about a forty-five-kilometer drive from St-Eustache, and the trip there is one that I undertake for weekly special shops rather than for the daily staple *va-et-vient* shopping. I also make an occasional visit on those alternate Thursdays when the market features as an adjunct or annex a section of stalls selling bric-a-brac and alleged antiques—generally and as it were congenitally overpriced, but not without the lurking possibility of a not wholly unamusing *trouvaille.* My cherished mid-nineteenth-century *escritoire* was one such find, its long years concealed at the far end of a chicken coop having lent it a perceptible odor which diminished its price at the stall of the "foreigner"—a Parisian refugee from advertising who emigrated south two decades ago—from whom I purchased it. The chicken smell was subdued by several heretical coats of varnish. ("With domestic objects, if you can't *use* them, they aren't beautiful, by definition"—a maxim of my brother's with which I am in rare assent.) As I began my stroll up the central aisle of the food market, I passed on my left M. Robluchon's mushroom stand with its first crop of late-summer treasures—I had missed the morel season this year, a subject about which the compact stallholder, his lack of centimeters appearing to be as much part of professional equipment as his wicker basket and his trufflehound, had amiably joshed me. On the right was the stall run by the sullen Mme Volois, the telltale small slovenlinesses in the presentation of her goods—a cabbage tumbled out of its overfull container into the basket of carrots below, a *mâche* (lettuce) lurking among the arugula like a misfiled letter—betraying the fact that this was the least satisfactory of the market's eight or nine vegetable stalls. As I began this perambulation I had a sense that today's quest would not be in vain, a hunter's keen premonition of success. This feeling grew as I passed M. Dupont's impeccable fruit stall (the strawberries long gone, the citrus fruits in their full pomp) and the cheese stand run by Mme Carpentier, a widow whose husband had performed all the "front of house" operations while he was alive, claiming the credit for the excellence of the cheeses and the perfection of the condition in which they were served, and causing all the locals to predict disaster when he died of a stroke, whereupon the almost entirely silent Mme Carpentier took over the public aspects of the stall and the quality of cheeses on sale if anything increased, the local *on-dit* soon switching from "She'll never make a go of it" to "Of course, it was she who had the nose all along."

The stalls were busy, this being quarter past eleven or so, and the market's fully operational period running from eight o'clock through to around twelve, when it would begin to wind down, often surprising unwary Anglo-Saxons and Northerners in general with the acceleration from one or two stallholders beginning to stow their wares to the moment when the market would seem as definitively abandoned and closed for business as a two-day-old Bedouin encampment, this applying especially to the produce section of the *marché;* among the antique dealers one or two would linger into the early afternoon before loading their trinkets and pieces into a compendious anthology of Peugeots, Renaults, and Citroëns of assorted vintages.

"The *merinjana* were satisfactory, monsieur?" called out M. Androuët as I joined the end of the dignified queue for his vegetable stall. Of course, my presence there was in itself a resounding affirmative. The aubergines—the Breton-born M. Androuët, known as an enthusiast for antiquities and for Provençal history, had used the dialect term, which I had taken effortlessly in my stride—had indeed been satisfactory, forming the basis for a superb ratatouille which had lasted me for several days, proving especially effective when served hot on a cold baguette or vice versa. (I was taught this form of sandwich by my brother in I think a unique instance of my culinary practice being influenced by his. The secret is to go easy on the tomato.) The other interesting dish giving *merinjana* a starring role is the subtly spiced Turkish *imam bayaldi,* the name meaning "the imam fainted," one is always told because the dish was so exquisite, though I have some-times wondered if an allergic reaction was also involved. The variety of allergic reactions and responses to toxins is surprising, ranging from the near-instantaneous swell-ing, blotching, and swooning of routine food allergies (I once saw a man in a restaurant in Strasbourg turn purple and have a seizure within thirty seconds of eating a peanut) to the seventy-two-hour asymptomatic period which precedes the delayed, invariably fatal, hepatic col-lapse induced by certain fungi.

I scanned the market. My scalp was itching slightly. (How little we would resent our itches if we took them for what they so often are—the ambassadors of resurgent life.) M. Androuët had dismissed his previous clients with dispatch to get to me, one of his very favorite customers. I purchased some salad potatoes, a few beans, carrots for color and texture, and plum tomatoes, before charmingly accepting a complimentary handful of basil, and cau-tiously adding my acquisitions to the eggs already nestled in the bottom of my shopping basket. M. Androuët would not sell me peppers as he said their condition was adequate but not exceptional. This was in part a joke about or an allusion to the incident that had advanced our relationship in the first place, when I had complained about some "woody" leeks he sold me and we had had words, a drama which culminated in my brandishing an evidentiary leek in, I later realized, unconscious imitation of Shakespeare's Fluellen, while we had the following exchange:

M. ANDROUËT: It is adequate.

ME: Mere adequacy is never adequate.

M. Androuët sneered and turned away, as I in my turn pivoted and marched off. And the next time I visited his stall we met on terms of greatly enhanced cordiality, eventually ripening into real friendship—a progression I have often noticed with the French, who seem to feel more comfortable with relationships that are preceded by and underpinned with an argument. (No accident that it's a French word: *entente.*)

The Thursday market was even busier than usual. I moved down the thronged aisle, delivering a quasi-accidental blow with my knee to the temple of a child who had been caroming noisily around the stalls; he stood stock still for a moment before bursting into abrupt hot tears. The shade yielded by the lime trees in the center of the square was becoming increasingly ineffective in the face of the day's full heat, which did however bring with it the consoling intimation of lunch.

Does the hunter always foresense his success? Is the successful arrowshot premonitioned down the length of the bowman's arm? Are rhetorical questions the pattern of all our seeking? As I headed into the market that day I confess I felt a chemical certainty as to the outcome of my expedition—a burgeoning knowledge as full of itself as a plumbline is confident of its own verticality. This grew in me, an edgy rising excitement, an intellectual tumescence, as I turned the corner past M. Remoulé's fruit stall, its selection of grapefruit in four different shades being especially colorful and bright this morning, his perfumed Cavaillon melons stacked beside the copious deliquescence of a display watermelon, sliced to exhibit its ripeness in a candid vulval gash; and around the bicycle-powered stall, as rickety and as ingenious as the first catamaran, where Mme Berti (an emigré Italian) sold the sorbets and ices she made herself at home before puffing the two and three-quarters kilometers into the square biweekly, never offering more than three of her famous ices (and shamingly generous to me, merely for having breathed the suggestion that subsequently mushroomed into a particularly successful flavor, the exquisitely refreshing elderflower sorbet—*mon anglais ingenieux,* was how she shy-makingly insisted on referring to me, to the admiring and envious audience of fellow-customers); and past the first outcroppings of the antiques market, underfurnished stalls whose very naiveté and improvisedness gave the connoisseur a comfortable sense that rarities there had an outside chance of being found; into the crowded heart of the market, its air of quiet avarice and mutual exploitation almost as visible as would be the heat waves rising off the road on my homeward journey, the effect enhanced by a healthy turnout of fleeceable tourists in holiday clothes, toward one group of whom I walked, ears so keenly pricked and eyes so peeled that I felt for a moment a sharp sense of our proximity to the animal kingdom, dependent on its senses as we have become on our wits—I could gather berries, eat the flesh of animals I had killed and cooked on a fire I had built with my own hands, with wood I had hewed myself—I was as you can tell in quite a state; only to find that the voices I had heard speaking English were not English but American; and then I pressed on to the far end of the market, past the herb stall whose hirsute proprietor was said to dispense some items for other than strictly culinary purposes (my brother once confided that marijuana "does nothing for me apart from make me feel randy as a goat at the time and unable to remember my own phone number the next morning"); and as I walked toward the antique stalls I could feel rising inside me the sense of disappointment that is often the immediate preliminary to success, the success I had striven for since grimy Portsmouth, the success which had involved me in several hundred miles' worth of pursuit and surveillance, so that I was deeply and shockingly gratified by the sight of her standing in front of me like a risen sun, her portly pale husband inevitably and glumly in attendance, she radiant, luminous, her hair emitting more light than it took in, her expression as she replaced a gilded oblong clock on the barrow one of restrained amusement and wry self-censoring politeness, the rebuffed stallholder, clearly besotted, keeping the ruined moonscape of his acne-pitted visage stoically empty, as she started to straighten up and move in my direction and I preemptively closed the space toward her—the other occupants of the market unreal to me, everything in the world a masquerade except me and her and my purposes, as I rose up before her and crisply announced:

"But my dears—how too, too unlikely!"

A Breakfast

And then we went to see those paintings of the disciples at Kerneval, the ones with the tools of the trade, which I'd only ever seen in reproduction before, and then we went down to near Chinon on the Loire where there's that sculpture park he made that there was all the fuss about, but the guidebook had given the wrong closing times so we had to kill a day looking at châteaux and so on and then go back, which was well worth it, wasn't it darling, and then a couple more days just pottering about, which I think Hugh found quite a relief as a break from looking at your brother's work even though he's almost as big a fan as I am, and then we drove down over the massif, which was amazing, and now we've just got three days left so we're going to look at the stuff in the small museum in Arles in his old house before dropping the car at Marseille and flying home, though Hugh isn't much looking forward to that because he's shit-scared of flying, aren't you darling?"

The question coincided with the hapless swain's ingestion of a *tartine*, so we were mercifully spared any reply other than an eager-to-please "humorous" wagging of the head. We were breakfasting on the patio, the time of morning still keeping us in the plane tree's shade; I had told my new guests, who would be staying the night, that they should arrive early enough to enjoy the morning view over the compact relief-map of rock and olive and vine, with the sun fiery on the hilltop town of Gordes, about five miles away.

"Admirably purposeful of you to combine business with pleasure so seamlessly," I roguishly averred, "though of course is there not a sense in which all honeymoons by definition merge business and pleasure?"

"That's something Duchamp gets so well in *The Bride Stripped Bare by Her Bachelors Even*—the intrusion of mechanization into areas where the dominant official metaphor is still that of intimacy. I think what Duchamp is saying is that the collapse of private space can be compared to the demise of the traditional systems of valorizing art, as well of course as the crisis in relations between the sexes under capitalism. Absolutely. I thought about doing my Ph.D. on Duchamp. In fact I was once offered a job in California teaching the history of avant-garde art. I think I told you that. Did your brother ever talk about Duchamp?"

"Hywl, you may find this fig confiture especially apt with that brioche. Best use for figs, in my view, especially since D. H. Lawrence's embarrassing comparison with female genitalia—though you honeymooners won't want to hear all this smutty talk from an old codger such as myself. Italian friends do say that figs are the ideal accompaniment to Parma ham. These of course are from one's own tree. Laura, spot more coffee? *Dommage.* No, I think Bartholomew thought that Duchamp should have stuck to chess. But let's not talk about dreary old work things, there'll be plenty of time for that later. I have promised you your formal interview and your formal interview you shall have. That's always assuming that Hywl will permit, of course—"

"I've got my book and your pool, I don't think there'll be any trouble passing the time till nightfall," he said, with a quick look at Laura that contained, I'm repulsed to say, the minutest flicker of a marital leer.

"And then I'm going to feed you up properly," I went on firmly. "Just a snack at lunchtime, because we poor drudges have got work to do and we don't want you getting stomach cramps in the pool and drowning, do we Hywl? but we'll have something a little more substantial in the evening and then I'll pack you off in the A.M. after a teensy snackette."

"You're much too k—"

"But perhaps first I should run over a few general sort of *thingies,* one doesn't like to call them rules but I suppose that's what they are. Be careful in the shallow end of the pool towards the left—the edge of the step is sharp enough to cut and we don't want to have to run you to the *médecin* for a typhus jab and miss valuable interviewing time, do we? Also, beware of apparently drowned wasps, many of which retain the capacity to sting. Perhaps indeed the ability to sting while appearing to be dead can be said to be what gives the acronym WASP its metaphoric applicability. Just a thought. In any case there is an expedient sort of net-like scoop which is also useful for getting rid of any floating leaves. I'm afraid I insist on feet being dried before swimmers return into the house— Laura will have noticed the design of the kilim just inside the door though only someone who has dabbled in carpet connoisseurship can be expected fully to appraise its rarity and value. I think there are some spare flip-flops in the shed, though I'm less confident as to whether we have any in your size, Hywl, as your feet seem to be remarkably large. If you feel the need for refreshment please remember *mi casa es su casa,* in other words you can make it for yourself, but if you want a cup of tea please note that the automatic ignition on the gas stove is not absolutely reliable. Lastly and most importantly, if you go for a walk up rather than down the hill towards the village, when you come to a fork in the road do not under any circumstances take the higher route, which will appear to (as indeed it does) take you into the village more quickly than the lower and rougher track, that so dispiritingly begins by dipping and causing one to lose some of the height one has so laboriously acquired, especially, Hywl, if one is showing the smidgeonest sign of being a pound or two overweight; but don't for any reason take the higher route, which goes through the land of two brothers who are absolute darlings except when they have shotguns in their hands and are out on their own property. There was a ghastly misunderstanding a few years ago with an English neighbor who used to pop over here to use the pool, not always *entre nous* with the most explicit of formal invitations having been issued first. So remember that it's *'round* the hill not *over* it. Right, that's about all. Lunch at one-ish. After that, well I know how much sleep you honeymooners need, so I'll let you off for a couple of hours, Laura, while Hywl and I drive into town to pick up a few essentials for supper, and then we'll interview again for the rest of the afternoon."

Coup d'oeil—no accident that's a French term.

Noisy Hywl then went off to unpack and generally crash around the house while I efficiently cleared up and Laura momentarily basked. One of the difficulties of correct breakfasting is to strike the appropriate balance between refreshment and satiation. Breakfast habits vary widely among cultures, and national attitudes to few subjects vary as much as they do over this. The Mexican laborer, rising at dawn to dunk a piece of *churro* in his coffee, swallow a gulp of spirits, and hie himself to his place of toil; the upright Frenchman at the *zinc* with his bowl of café au lait and his optional croissant; the trenchermanly Victorian, with his kipper, his kedgeree, his marmalady toast, and his mutton chop; the Australian drover, in enigmatic harmony with the hot-tempered gaucho of the distant Argentinian pampas under the same Southern sky, commemorating the sunrise (breaking, in one's imagination, over a quasi-Martian red landscape of rock and sand) with steak, eggs, and ketchup; or Casanova, breakfasting on two hundred oysters before commencing the real business of the day, seduction or librarianship (there being, perhaps, an unacknowledged continuity between the two pursuits, something to do with the essence of cataloguing); the Japanese, with his unimaginable soup; the horse-borne dawn libations of the Mongols, opening a vein in their horses' necks to suck therefrom the strengthening blood; the inventive, terrible breakfastings of nomads on steppe, desert, and mountain pass. My brother, typically, was an enthusiast of the "fry-up," or—as he insisted on calling it, in homage to his time in Dublin, when he claims to have acquired this particular taste—the FIB: Full Irish Breakfast. I ate this meal with him in many a drear café, not to mention the dusty but well-lit studios and ateliers where he never failed to install a stove (frequently illegal, usually gas-powered), on which he would cook his bacon-egg-sausage and fried-bread combinations (dependable black pudding being more problematic to obtain and therefore *à volonté*), pronouncing the ingredients as if they were one word, baconeggsausagefriedslice. He was fond of claiming that anyone who could "do a proper fry-up" had mastered the essential skills of time-and-ingredient management necessary to prepare any other dish: "Compared to a FIB, Veal 'Prince Orloff' with *pommes de terre soufflés* is a doddle." My own preference is for a piece or two of well-chosen fruit and a cup of coffee; animal fats and cereals are respectively too indigestible and too dispiriting for matutinal consumption. Sometimes a croissant is in order, though that depends on whether there is a sufficiently high-quality boulangerie in the area. At my home in Provence it depends on whether I can be bothered to nip into town for the daily shop before otherwise breaking my fast; I usually can't summon up sufficient inclination. Today's croissants and *tartines* were a concession to tubby Hywl.

"Shall we begin?" I startled Laura by asking. She sat up, her baggy shorts moving down over the top of her gilded knees as she did so.

"It's so nice here, it makes you not want to work. I wonder if I'd get anything done if I lived down here."

"One gets over that."

A gecko, galvanized by the rising heat, flickered over the patio table between us. Laura began arranging various notebooks and technical aids, producing them from a capacious, artistic-looking raffia shoulderbag.

"Perhaps, Mr. Winot, if you could give me a rough summary of your and B.W.'s upbringing, in order to . . ."

"B.W.?"

"Sorry, your brother—that's how I've been referring to him in my notes. To avoid for the moment the problem I'm going to have when I actually get to the point of writing the biography, of whether to call him Barry, which feels a bit chummy, or Winot, which is a bit public school. So I decided that I'm not going to decide until I actually begin writing."

"I hope and trust that I am Tarquin throughout. Tarquin Tarquinibus, the Tarquin of Tarquins. As you probably know I was christened Rodney; the Tarquin was a stroke of my own, influenced by Shakespeare's charismatic villain. Ha ha. What a bore Lucrece is—all that virtue, all that wailing. A rough summary of our upbringing. No, I don't think I'll do that. But if you ask me specific questions I'll give you specific answers."

I would not be giving my interlocutor full credit if I did not register here both her momentary taken-abackness and her quick recovery from it, like a crack regiment summoned back from a frontier war to suppress an insurrection in the capital. The noise of cicadas made a sudden unbidden impact on my attention, one of those abrupt transitions from the territories beneath the threshold of consciousness to those far above it, hurtling like a rocket-powered lift from deep unheededness to irritating unignorability.

"O.K.," she said, with some attractively business-like rearranging of papers. "Tell me about your and your brother's education."

Thoughtful Tarquin gazed handsomely into the distance for a moment or two.

"I prefer not to chronicle my early development in terms of externalities. In this respect the imperatives of the biographer and the lived life of the subject are at odds.

After all, the dreary chronicle of schools, awards, laundry lists—what do these tell us about the felt subjectivity? Perhaps, indeed, the laundry list has more of the subject's subjectivity than does the other dreary documentary paraphernalia—more quirkiness, more aleatory individuation. Can our hero really have gone a whole week without changing his underpants, only to have changed them twice a day for the next trimester? What use can he conceivably have had for that embroidered dress shirt which we are told on this receipt—with its strangely beautiful handwriting suggesting to our imaginative historian's novelettish mind the possibility of a romance between the bashful blushing beauty behind the counter and the ruined giant of an artist-man presenting his bag of laundry to her on his weekly pilgrimage, a fleeting human contact on which he, without knowing it, has come to depend—has a 'permanent stain'? (A possible title for the biography?) Perhaps one day a writer will invent a life and present it simply in the form of a sequence of documents, without emphasis or commentary: birth certificate, school reports, driver's license, life insurance policy, requests for overdue library books, laundry lists, home contents insurance inventory, shopping lists, unfilled prescriptions, unredeemed petrol-station vouchers, a passport application filled out in a false name but never sent in, and a final sequence of bills from doctors and nursing agencies, climaxing with a startlingly high invoice from a fashionable mortician. Upon such a structure one could impose one's own consolatory fictions of achievement and development. On the one hand: to have done such deeds! On the other: to have paid such a price! And our own lives, by contrast: how boring, how riskless, and how very very preferable!

"To 'answer' your question, then, I was brought up by tutors, a process not so very different from having educated myself. My brother went to a series of public schools, supposedly educational mausolea of dwindling prestige to which he gave credit for his own absolute lack of interest in general culture, as well as for that rather tiresome pretense of classlessness he went on to adopt— 'all artists are working-class,' and all that nonsense. You will notice that I myself am refreshingly free from that affectation. Father eventually gave up on Bartholomew, or was persuaded to give up on him. I think my own obvious gifts and the sense of promise I have been told that I emanated was reassuring to Papa and allowed him to offer my brother more leeway; perhaps one success per family per generation is quite enough—anyway, Father let him go to the Slade, from where he performed the unusual feat of managing to be expelled. As for myself, I could say that a mere list of subjects studied and examinations passed, of tutors humbled and Loeb Library texts effortlessly ingested, would be of little bearing or import. Aren't the really eventful changes to do with one's feeling for certain textures, one's enduring preference for certain colors, an inchoate attraction to certain lines of poetry, certain buildings? The shadow under the eaves on the wall across from one's fourth-storey bedroom window as it changes through the seasons of the Parisian year. In terms of our inner lives, our *real* lives, what effect, after all, is had by the result of the Battle of Waterloo, compared to the question of whether or not to put Tabasco sauce on one's oysters?"

By now Hywl had finished whatever he had been up to in the house—no doubt he had not missed the opportunity to go rummaging Welshly through my effects—and was in the pool swimming lengths with an astonishing walrus-like profusion of gruntings, splashings, and puffings.

"Hugh was a swimming blue at Cambridge."

"Yes, I expect so."

Laura glanced toward her new husband, who now, with some sort of complicated self-inverting underwater turn, displaced what even by his standards was a prodigious amount of water. It was hard not to conclude that by the time he had finished there would be less liquid in the pool than there was outside it.

"Do you know why your brother was expelled from the Slade? Forgive me, it's just that there are so many stories."

"If you will in turn forgive *me* for saying so, it is unwise to permit the sun to fall so unmediatedly on the skin above one's knees. It is a place where cyclists in particular suffer the most fearsome burns. An adjustment of a foot or so to the left, whence the shade has treacherously migrated, and—just so. It was something to do with some practical escapade that went wrong—or was it something to do with stripping the lead from church roofs and melting it down—or perhaps he just got chucked out for not being very good. I'm afraid the details are a little blurred. At the time I was reading a lot of Valéry and having a series of dreams which seemed more real than waking life: certain passages in Rilke and Proust, certain poems of Leopardi and axioms of Lichtenberg, a certain bag of hot chestnuts eaten outside the Dominion Theatre on Tottenham Court Road two days before the winter solstice—these are what stand in for my own 'memories.' All I can really say that I remember of that period of my brother's life is a summer afternoon walk with the sound of a church bell blown across the Thames to the Lambeth side and then drowned out by the thrumming of a blue tugboat."

Laura sighed a sigh which spoke of difficulty and of collaboration; a similar noise might have been exchanged by Verdi and Boito.

"Your father had his ups and downs in business. Did these affect you much, as children? Were you very aware of them?"

"Nothing which reminds us of transience and impermanence can be regarded as wholly bad. We are all vagrants on the earth, we are all ultimately unhoused."

"What were the first signs of your brother's artistic interests, that you remember?"

"They tell me that there are certain specific moments which everybody in a generation can remember—wars, sporting triumphs, unpopular assassinations, moon-landings. At the same time there are moments which are supposed to be commemorated in each individual's life: early sexual encounters, car accidents, bereavements; for a specific generation of people of a certain age, the first time one saw a color television. This brutal colonization of interior life has no interest for me nor, I suspect, for most true artists. I am more interested in the things I cannot remember, in absences, elisions, vacuities, negativities, voids, aporiae, nothingness. My own consciousness of my own artistic vocation came to me in one such moment, when I took a papier-mâché model my brother had made of an elephant, trunk erect and unconvincing mahout and all, and rode my tricycle backwards and forwards over it."

"When was that?"

"I'm not sure—I don't remember precisely. About quarter to four, I think. Certainly before teatime. That's when my act was discovered. I am misunderstanding your question on purpose to make a point."

"What happened?"

" 'Mixed reviews.' Much as one would expect. Great rage and pain. One was rather in the doghouse momentarily. But artists can't expect to have undifficult childhoods. Can I freshen that glass of iced tea for you? No? We had a nanny who was kind to me but who shortly thereafter had to be sacked and things quietened down a bit then."

"What was your parents' attitude to your brother's beginnings as an artist?"

"Heavens—anyone would think you were writing my brother's biography. Ha, ha. Mother and Father were always somewhat inscrutable about these things but I think that like everyone else they regarded my brother's stuff as a bit of a joke. My mother, who had been something of an actress, understood the artistic nature, and saw of course that I was much closer to it—I think she had a great respect for my inwardness, though of course she went to enormous pains never to show it and to pretend to like Bartholomew's stuff—she could be very subtle and thoughtful, my mother, in that way. Father would just say 'Well done, boys' whenever either of us did anything."

"Could you describe any other intellectual influences on your childhood? Did living abroad have any impact?"

"Jewish mystics believe that God created human beings because He loves stories. Did you know that? The words we use to describe the inner life are so coarse, aren't they? Impact, influence, development. It's as if the soul were a small, contentious province in the Balkans, sandwiched between two greater powers. Paris is a certain texture of the light, recorded in some paintings by Gustave Caillebotte. Stockholm is the sight of a virgin snowfield, uncanceled by human feet. Dublin is a malty smell, a regret, a glimpse of dampened sawdust."

"Notwithstanding your reservations about influence, were there any tutors you remember in particular? In other words, as a biographer, is there anything I should know about formative influences on your brother that otherwise I probably won't?"

"I expect that's a politely indirect way of asking me about my perfect French. We had a perceptive young Frenchman called Etienne who visited us during the holidays for a few years, mostly in London and Norfolk. He was quick to see a streak of genius in me and encouraged me a lot in my quiddity, in my me-ness. Bartholomew he encouraged with a hysterical heartiness that didn't convince anybody—'This boy is going to be the greatest sculptor since Michelangelo,' all that sort of thing."

"Do you know where I might be able to find Etienne now?" Laura asked with, for the first time in the conversation, a note of alacrity. I could see the pulse in her lovely throat.

"It is *so* relieving to be able to give an immediately affirmative answer. He's in Père-Lachaise Cemetery, in one of those hideous nineteenth-century family mausolea. His family was much, much posher than we suspected. For a generally voluble people the French have many unguessed reticences—but I expect you knew that. I don't remember the family name but I expect I could find it for you somewhere—Gagnaire, perhaps, I think."

"What happened?"

"Bee sting—poor Etienne had an allergy, long before they were fashionable. And then the unlucky chap turned out to have run out of antidote. Or rather he injected himself, because they found a puncture mark, but there wasn't a trace of the antidote in his body. It was as if the syringe had been emptied and replaced with something else—water or a saline solution. He used to carry it about with him everywhere. We weren't with him when he died—he'd gone to Kew for the day. It took about half an hour, apparently. To die, that is, not to go to Kew. Etienne would say how absurd it was to have to regard something called a 'bumblebee'—you can imagine how that sounded in his accent—as potentially fatal."

"Were you close to any of the servants?"

As she spoke I momentarily saw Mitthaug's face as he lay on the rails before the onrushing train. He was looking up at me with an expression of surprise so pure that it would in another context have been comic.

"Not especially. There was the Irish servant girl I mentioned, and a Norwegian interested in pickles who went under a District Line underground train—he taught my brother to make papier-mâché sculptures, largely I think as a way of occupying him so that he could spend more time with me. He used to make *gravlax,* the cured salmon dish whose national origin is so ungrippingly disputed among the Scandinavian countries. *Grav* means 'buried,' by the way, and is etymologically related to the English 'grave.' The technique of curing fish in salt, sugar, pepper, and dill is adaptable: *gravad makrel* is an especially interesting variant, though it is important that the mackerel be fresh, since its high natural level of oil means that it goes off rapidly and pungently—one reason why it was the only foodstuff that could be legally sold within the city of London on Sundays. I can let you have a recipe. Gooseberry sauce also goes well with mackerel."

"Did your brother ever come here? He didn't live far away, did he, in Arles? Did you ever visit him there? When did you buy this place?"

It was time to look at my watch. From the corner of my eye I could see that Hywl had unfolded a deckchair and was seat-bulgingly, but with a welcome lack of noisiness, settling to the task of giving himself skin cancer.

"I'm going to have to start making preparations for luncheon—chopping vegetables, that sort of thing. We can chat a little while I potter about. If that isn't too domestically blissful seeming for a thrustful young woman such as yourself."

Laura grimaced her assent. Balzac, the largest and most even-tempered of the St-Eustache cats, padded past into the kitchen. The day stretched in front of us.

A Barbecue

Arson is perhaps the most literal-minded of all violent crimes. Who has not, on passing some large public masterpiece of architecture, or glimpsing an exquisitely ordered and human domestic interior through a ground-floor window (the sheet music open on the piano, the steepling bookcases and expectant hearth) felt an uncomplicated urge to set fire to them? Of all the Emperor Nero's amusing and instructive misdeeds—the collapsing bedroom with which he attempted to murder his mother, the forcing of audiences to hear his execrable singing—it is the burning of Rome which has the satisfying quality of an archetypal act. How many of the great fires of history,

London in 1666, Chicago in 1871, might have been caused, not by the dreary happenstance of an overturned cooking pot or an unwatched kettle, but through that genuine overflowing of animal high spirits which expresses itself in arson?

It is this fundamental impulse which, I would suggest, underlies the popularity of the barbecue. (The etymology of "barbecue" is *vaut le détour:* the word derives from the Haitian *barbacado,* a rack-frame system used to suspend off the ground such items as beds. We may conjecture the device's use as an instrument of torture or cannibalism. *Maïs,* the Haitian goddess of life, from whose name one derives the word 'maize,' seems to be the only other term to have metamorphosed from the one language to the other, changing shape while retaining its essential identity like a Greek god disguising himself for the purposes of seduction or punishment.) No, the act of setting fire is a deep human imperative that continues to be celebrated in the potent suburban ritual of charcoal briquettes and lighter fluid—a direct link with man's ancestral past, with the magical acts of painting, followed by hunting, followed by an open fire, followed by the tribal feast on freshly killed mammoth-flesh, paralleling the composition of the shopping list, the expedition to the supermarket, the barbecue itself, and the ceremonial male feat of dismemberment or, as it is quaintly known, "carving."

For my own purposes I like to barbecue on a permanent site, preferably one constructed of bricks with adaptable flues providing ventilation; I have built such an object at

St-Eustache, with my own fair hands. This sits at the other side of the kitchen from the main patio and the *piscine* (which looks out toward the olive groves and hill village of Gordes); instead the small patioed area overlooks a wider panorama of vines and foothills gradually rising in the direction of the Lubéron.

That evening, after a long day's journey into interview, I made my barbecue preparations. In front of Laura's admiring gaze, I spread the charcoal (a lucrative sideline of the local *garagiste*) and cunningly plunged into it an electric fire-starter, similar to in design, but psychologically very distinct from, the immersion devices used to heat single cups of hot water in tragic bedsits.

"I can't abide the smell of chemicals imparted by those horrid little brick jobs," I explained forcefully.

"We don't get the chance to barbecue in London. Partly we can't be bothered, and then there's the pollution and the pigeons and the neighbors' ghetto-blaster—it's just not worth it. And the weather's not predictable enough, which is also the case at my parents' place in Derby—they've got a built-in barbecue which they never use. Anyway, Hugh says barbecuing gives him performance anxiety."

"No such worries for some of us," I smoothly ventured. "This will take about seven and a half minutes to get going and another forty or so before I can start cooking the food. Apéritif? Or we can continue this flattering inquisition."

"There's something I've been wondering, before we knock off for the day—why are you talking to me now?

I've asked you several times and been to see you three times, and you could have agreed to talk at any time, so why now? If you don't mind my asking."

"We speak so casually of motives, don't we? I'd prefer not to say more than that. What would have happened had you asked Nero or Caligula or Tiberius about their reasons? We circle around ourselves like planets orbiting the sun."

Slight pause here. My darling has what poker players call a "tell"—a physical indication which betrays the commensurate psychic effort involved in uttering an untruth. Movingly, her tell is one of the most banal and most common: she looks down. The perversity of love is such that I found this far more thrillingly exotic than the most volcanic, shoulder-cricking twitch.

"O.K.—so why don't we go back to the question about why you moved down here."

"The principles of barbecuing are not complicated," I explained. "The art is an ancient one: indeed a barbecue takes place in the *Iliad,* when the Trojans slay a sheep described as being of 'silvery whiteness' before cutting the meat up into smaller pieces, spitting them, and taking them away from the fire when well roasted—a process instantly recognizable as the shish kebab which has been Turkey's defiant contribution to the rapid cuisines of the West. I note in passing that the historical Troy is located in present-day Turkey, a good cheap country to holiday in if your husband's earning power should fail to live up to expectations. The coals are mounted up in a pyramid sufficiently high to provide approximately a two-inch bed when spaced out and disassembled; this action is performed when the coals are covered in gray ash. Forty minutes or so. Nothing could be simpler. At the same time one needs to remember and respect the different natures of the ingredients being prepared: fish requiring more delicate treatment (basting, even the utilization of indirect heat) than meat, steaks requiring an optimum thickness so as to retain their juices while not charring on the outside—in practice, somewhere between one and three inches. Spatchcocked chicken (chicken *en crapaudine,* like a toad), butterflied lamb, vegetable kebabs, brochettes, grilled sea bass. My brother used to say that cooking could teach the importance of respecting the diversity of materials, a crucial lesson to remember when it comes to working with stone. I would add that autumn or mid- to late summer, like now, is the best time of year for barbecuing, when the whole experience—the crackling fire, the dancing smoke, the stars themselves—has an elegiac note, summer leaving to join the queue of other summers on the return trip to urban life, reality, home, marriage. I first came down here when I visited my brother, liked it, and bought a house in the area after my parents died."

I deftly extracted the glowing fire-starter from the bottom of the mound of incandescing charcoal.

"Would it be a fearsome bore to nip over to the poolside and collect hubby? It's time for a sundowner. We can keep talking, I'm sure he won't mind."

"Right."

Did I detect a small hint of irritation at my demonstrable mastery of the situation? No matter: time for champagne. While I adroitly maneuvered the cork from the bottle (I'm afraid the precise marque will have to be my little secret—we don't want to start a run on stocks and put the price up, now do we?), Hywl damply arrived from the vicinity of the pool, a towel draped around his neck, his moistened leg-hairs a secondary sexual characteristic in themselves.

"I'll just nip upstairs and change," he said wetly in both senses.

"Capital."

She came back from the pool carrying her forgetful spouse's pair of unintelligent-person's black sunglasses. I handed her a glass of champagne with wordless intimacy. The barbecue was giving off nicely smarting smoke.

"You know, I'm really a very wicked man."

"How so?"

"In my flat in London I have a real fire. Notwithstanding my admiration for the 1956 Clean Air Act, an unusually successful piece of legislation but one that does prohibit the ignition of carbon fuels for the purposes of domestic heating in the capital, I find that civilized life in Britain in the winter months is impossible without spending a substantial number of one's evenings in the company of crackling logs. There are some laws, however acknowledgedly excellent in their social functioning, which one just can't take seriously as applying to oneself, don't you find?"

"I often feel that way about speed limits."

"Who was it said that the maxim of French intellectual life was *priorité à la gauche?* Perhaps it was me. Stuffed olive?"

"Er—I'm all right, thanks."

"You asked about my move down here. We both know that was a tactful way of asking about the death of my parents. Freud remarks somewhere that it is humanly impossible to come to terms with the full extent of the randomness, luck, and accident involved in life. I found that a comforting thought when I was younger, though I have always felt that the great man underestimated the role of malignity in human affairs. No, I bought this property fifteen years ago in the aftermath of our parents' death: I was sole beneficiary of their estate, which I think can reasonably be taken as sufficient proof that I was their favorite, notwithstanding the various fusses made over my sibling, who was at that point making a very substantial living from his lumps and blobs and wouldn't have needed any of the money anyway. I spent the inheritance partly on rebuilding the cottage in Norfolk, badly damaged in the original incident of course, and the remainder on purchasing this property from a Belgian who had retired down here but was now moving back to the old country, largely, the village thought, as a way of punishing his wife, who had developed an allergy to olive oil. There was enough left over to build the pool and the rest, judiciously invested, provides the modest annual stipend with which I eke out my days, my needs.

"The accident in which my parents perished, not perhaps the correct verb, took place in our country cottage, the one in fact which you once so delightfully (to me anyway) visited. My parents had been away for a week, my father on business, my mother as a way of gratifying her itch to travel. John Donne remarks somewhere that the urge to knowledge is the most ungovernable of all the passions. He never met my mother, or he would have known that it can be vied with by simple restlessness. But. In their absence, 'inexplicably' as the coroner put it, they had left all the gas taps on in the kitchen, a circumstance which would not have been dangerous in itself had it not coincided with a bona fide and full-scale leak from the gas boiler, situated in that alcove under the stairs which I now use as a distinctly modest wine cellar—you may remember that gratifyingly chocolaty Château La Lagune 1970 I fetched thence on the occasion of your trip. My father had said something about a gas leak and I, as I testified at the inquest—I'm afraid one rather 'broke down,' but the coroner was so sweet about it, and you know how notoriously fierce they can be—had arranged for the plumber to come (Mr. Perks, who testified at the inquest, too) but had arranged it for the subsequent week, the week after my parents' return—not understanding the urgency of the situation, and being due myself to return to a series of pressing engagements in the capital. I myself had a key and free access to the house so although I had left a day before Mama and Papa I could certainly have come back at any time and met the same fate. 'You are, in a sense, a very lucky man,' said the coroner—I'm afraid one rather broke down at that, too. Anyway my father came in and, in the final component of this multiplying series of mishaps, each of them necessary but not sufficient for the ultimate catastrophe, moved into the hallway, where the first light bulb appears not to have been working, and then, my mother following, as was her wont, immediately behind, he went to turn on the light in the hall beside the boiler, just adjacent to the maximum concentration of gas. Tragically, the lightswitch turned out to be sparky, malfunctioning, and so, not to put too fine a point on it—kaboom."

"I'm sorry."

"Yes. I think I can honestly claim to be a storm-tossed orphan of the tempest. Bartholomew was upset, too, though of course he did always have that certain robustness. He was quite helpful about rebuilding the cottage, gave advice about cheap materials and so on. It was a good excuse to get rid of the thatching, which as all Norfolk residents know makes home insurance prohibitively expensive. Ah, the fortunate bridegroom emerges from his chamber."

Slow Hywl had indeed thudded downstairs during the last three or four sentences. I flourishingly poured him a glass of champagne and gestured expansively in the direction of one of the rattan chairs (which live outside during the good weather).

"This is a great place—how long have you had it?" asked subtle Hywl. Laura and I caught each other's eye momentarily in shared suppression of an identical smile.

"My parents' death is not a subject I choose to discuss quotidianly, let alone biquotidianly, if that means twice a day. I have never been entirely clear as to whether bi-monthly, biannually mean every two months and years or twice a month, year, have you? Laura—more 'poo?"

"I'm sure that Hugh didn't mean to upset you, Mr. Winot."

"No, I—"

"I can't remember whether or not I told you about one in particular of my abandoned projects, Laura. This was before I came to the realization we discussed in Norfolk about incomplete work being superior to complete (because, dear boy, more suggestive, more evocative, more authentically in resonance with the texture of experience in this century) moving logically thence to the conclusion that unrealized or preferably uncommenced work is duly superior in its turn. 'I am re-begot / Of absence darkness, death; things which are not.' John Donne, who needless to say didn't take his own hint, as artists so often fail to do. I had in mind a project for a novel which would begin in the usual manner, the usual dreary scene-setting and establishment of character, except that gradually the characters' identities would begin to slip and to blur, and so would the geographical surroundings. The figure who began as the upright butler suffering secret night terrors would appear to be metamorphosing into the lord of the manor's sideburn-wearing eldest son, proud of his collection of Hawaiian shirts and of the time he drove a Jaguar into the swimming pool, causing his father to remark on being told the news: 'Has the poor beast drowned?' The set-piece description of the village fête, annual scene of rivalries over frocks, giant marrows, and the vicar's attention, takes on characteristics of a Finnish celebration of the longest day of the year, when the children are allowed to stay up all hours and confused owls fly through the unyielding twilight, and then metamorphoses again into a spontaneous street party in an English seaside town, where the unprecedented fall of heavy and settling snow turns the scene into a Dutch painting, and citizens hub-bub among the palm trees and frost-smothered motor vehicles in the suddenly trafficless and civilized streets. The nature of the characterizations would alter, too: the village doctor, a tired honorable man, no longer sure of the promises offered by his profession or of what he has always been frightened to see underlying beneath it— specifically, his sense of vocation: a figure being por-trayed in the round, completely, inwardly, perceptively, in-depth, would slowly change, become stiff and carica-tured, a character familiar from a thousand accounts of the 'male menopause' and mid-career angst, and at the same time his own responses would coarsen, grow more and more bluff, his conversation now a series of pep talks, precepts, one-liners, and single entendres, while his prac-tice would simultaneously and mysteriously transpose itself from Suffolk to inner-city Cardiff. At the same time the village milkman, a conventional philanderer of the most profoundly familiar depiction, would slowly, via a chance perusal of an article in a pornographic magazine, develop an interest in tantric sexual techniques and therefrom a passionate concern with all aspects of Eastern wisdom, gradually becoming a student of Buddhism proper, deepeningly fascinated by the magic practices of Tibet, while at the same time his timekeeping and industrious milkmanship becomes an industrywide legend. And so on. Only the style of the book would remain consistent, driving, forceful, its stable nature underlying the chaos and limitless mutability of everything else in the narrative—though it would no longer be clear if the book *was* a narrative since the essential mechanisms of propulsion, surprise, development, would seem largely to be forgotten. An initially lighthearted effect, comically incongruous and ingeniously pulled off, would grow in its intensity; gradually, as the stability of plot and character fell away, and all certainties became erased, the work would become more troubling, the undercurrent of emotion and anxiety both more forcefully present and at the same time more unclear, until the appalled readers, unable to understand what was happening either to them or to the story, and also unable to stop reading, would watch the wholesale metastasization of the characters into one another, the collapse of the very idea of plot, of structure, of movement, of self, so that when they finally put the book down they are aware only of having been protagonists in a deep and violent dream whose sole purpose is their incurable unease."

There was a conversational silence, underpinned by ratcheting cicadas. We were now lit only by fire and starlight. The *garagiste*'s nephew, on leave from his national service, was racing his notorious unsilenced motorcycle on the Gordes–Cavaillon road. A drop of basting juices fell off the sea bass and spluttered on the white charcoals. I could hear the not quite subliminal tinkling of bubbles in our crystal champagne flutes.

"Well now," I said. "This is very pleasant."

An Omelette

Early mornings are my favorite time of the day in Provence. The sensation of slightly *mouvementé* air, of the preliminary to a full breeze, and the sight of dew on the plants by kitchen, patio, and pool, like the crystalline cerulean sky that so often accompanies daybreak, never fail to lift the spirits.

That morning I padded downstairs at an impressive five minutes to six. There was a degree of ambient crispness in the kitchen (stone-flagged, I think I may have forgotten to say, and challengingly cool to bare feet all year 'round). I put the kettle on and stood leafing through my much stained paperback reprint of Reboul's *La Cuisinière*

Provençale (1895). As the kettle boiled, and was ultra-politely removed from the hob before starting to whistle, I made a large pot of Twinings English Breakfast which I decanted into my capacious thermos. Then I headed for the door, pausing only to pocket a peach and an orange from the fruit bowl as I went; all these preparations having acquired the agreeably staid pattern of a ritual from the fact that I repeat them on each and every one of the late summer and autumn mornings on which I choose to go mushroom hunting.

The car—my car this time, a thrifty Volkswagen, resident at St-Eustache all the year 'round, rather than any of the hire models mentioned hitherto, the last of which had been returned to the franchise concession at Avignon—had been parked an earshot-defying hundred yards or so from the honeymooners' bedroom. It started first time and I bumped along the unmetaled lane to the main road, before roaring off in the direction of the Lubéron hills. On the seat beside me were my wicker basket, my Sherlock Holmesian magnifying glass (hardly ever used or needed), and my copy of *Champignons de nos pays* by Henri Romagnesi (ditto, though I also keep all six volumes of *Champignons du Nord et du Midi* by André Marchand back at the house).

In the following account, the alert reader will notice that I am being a little bit coy about the geographical specifics. Forgive me, but we amateur mycologists, especially amateur mycologists of a culinary bent, passionately guard our favored patches of land—a promising batch of *cèpe*-yielding beeches here, a cropped roadside thronging with ink-caps there, yonder a patch of nettles known to feature spectacular examples of *Langermannia gigantea*, or the giant puffball, and somewhere else a field with a healthy quantity of cow excrement conducive to the fructation of the nasty tasting but currently popular hallucinogen *Psilocybe semilanceata,* appropriately known in English as the Liberty Cap. (This, by the way, is not, as it is sometimes taken to be, the hallucinogen used by the notorious shamans of the Koryk tribe in far Siberia, the *Amanita muscaria*, or fly agaric, ingestible via reindeer or indeed human urine, most often popularly reproduced in the image of a red-capped white-dotted toadstool, providing a convenient seat for any momentarily resting elf or fairy. The shamans call that mushroom the *Wapag,* after a body of magical beings who inhabit the fungi with a view to passing on secrets from the realm of the spirits.) We mushroom hunters are a secretive and wary breed, and it is through ingrained force of habit that I confine my account of the site of my labors to the description: *a patch of land somewhere in the south of France.* As evidence of the need for caution, the first car I encountered belonged to M. Robert, the local schoolmaster and a noted fungi enthusiast whose special passion, he had once divulged to me when we bumped into each other at Mme Cottison's stall in Cavaillon market, was the *cèpe.* His *deux-chevaux* was heading, interestingly and provocatively, in the opposite direction. As our vehicles passed each other the teacher and I both raised a hand in cautious fraternal salutation.

It's fascinating to remark how different are these excursions, undertaken in Provence and in Norfolk. Partly this is to do with dress: my multiply layered and woolly hatted autumnal East Anglian self could be taken for no relation to my linen-shirted meridional alter ego. In England I am a freak, participating in a bizarre act of voluntary self-endangerment; in France I am the intelligent *homme moyen sensuel* rationally maximizing the use of the earth's resources and my pleasure, and also saving a few francs in the process. The air in Provence (when the mistral is not blowing, of course, since that phenomenon makes the practice, indeed the very thought, of mycology impossible) carries the scent of wild herbs, of the *garrigue;* in Norfolk, on some days, before plunging into the deep English silence of the woods, I fancy I can catch the faintest tang of the sea. Please imagine here a passage which evokes the comparative experiences of mushroom hunting all over Europe, with many new metaphors and interesting facts.

I parked the car in a passing place and state-approved picnic spot some ten kilometers away from home—a hilly site (though not *too* hilly). Seizing basket and knife and leaving my other equipment—this being a specific quest rather than a generalized exploratory expedition, more like Captain Bligh's voyage than Captain Cook's—I set off boldly upward, my breath not even, at that hour, starting to steam as it would begin to in the next few weeks (and as it conceivably would already be doing had I been on a comparable expedition in Norfolk). The faint path wound along and up a rocky way through patchy conifers

233

in the direction of a grove of Mediterranean oak and beech, not directly visible from the roadside. Later in the year this would become a popular location for *la chasse,* especially for the massacre of those songbirds which always make disappointingly unmeaty eating. For the moment I had the landscape to myself. In the distance I could see the hill town of ———.

The walk took about twenty minutes. Mushroom hunting is an agreeable mixture of the active and the contemplative: on the one hand is the fresh air, the promise of the early day, the walk, the sudden bends and stoops; on the other the intellectual activity of identification and of what military strategists—in one of these euphemisms which often seem more compellingly sanguinary than the term it replaces—call "target acquisition." The atmosphere was described with a false jollity by Tolstoy in *Anna Karenina:* in truth it involves an anxious concentration on one's own performance, a determination to come back with one's mushroom or on it, a silent free-floating mixture of boredom and anxiety of the sort familiar to hunters and psychoanalysts. So much looking down can induce a vertigo when one finally looks up and realizes where one is, who one is. Comically, on this occasion I straightaway came across a robust clump of *cèpes* under the first two trees I examined—M. Robert would have been doing very well indeed if he had found anything remotely comparable. I enjoyed one of the pleasures of mycology, a brief silent rapturous gloat. On a different day with a different purpose I would have been delighted to find my mission accomplished so rapidly (I might even have shared some of my harvest with Pierre and Jean-Luc). Not today, though. I pressed on. At the edge of the clump I found a patch of *Entoloma sinuatum,* the toxic field mushroom look-alike known as *Le Grand Empoisonneur de la Côte d'Or,* not a fungus you often see in the United Kingdom. Again I pressed on.

I found what I was looking for almost exactly where I had thought I would.

"Well, well, sleepyheads," I said to the descending honeymooners, shuffling sleep- and sheep-facedly into the kitchen. "What sort of time do you call this?"

Gurgling pipes and offstage creakings had already warned me of that anticipated eventuality, The Rising of Hywl. The kettle was coming to the boil as I spoke. Was it my imagination, or had he managed to put on some weight overnight? Laura was wearing a white T-shirt and black-and-white checked pantaloons above a pair of maroon slippers, the whole ensemble creating an effect that was obscurely near-Eastern.

"Seventeen minutes past ten," she counterattacked firmly. "And it's all your fault for giving us such good food and drink last night, so don't try. Is that fresh coffee? Yes? God, I think I've died and gone to heaven."

"I'm a tea man, myself, first thing. I find coffee's effects on my nerves to be overly pronounced, when taken on an empty stomach. Balzac as you know undermined his constitution fatally by drinking forty or fifty cups of, in his case, literally poisonously strong black coffee daily. You will counterpropose that Hazlitt ruined his stomach by overindulging his affection for Chinese green tea. I have no answer. James Joyce exacerbated his stomach ulcer by drinking a Swiss white wine which, unbeknownst to him, contained significant traces of sulphur."

"The beds were very comfortable," ventured unliterary Hywl. I smiled patronizingly and depressed the plunger into the *cafetière*.

"Now you just sit yourselves down there and make yourselves at home. I've been up and about betimes and I've picked some wild mushrooms which I thought I'd make into a lovely omelette for the two of you, and then Laura and I can chat because I'm sure there are a few more things you'd like to know, and then you can be off on your way, to Arles is it?"

"Well, as you know, there are loads of things of your brother's there at his old house, including a whole lot of working sketches which they keep in the vaults and which I've got permission to see, but I'm afraid that there's a more immediate problem which is that we can't have your omelette because Hywl doesn't eat eggs."

An involuntary sound of dismay escaped me.

"But but but that's impossible. Everybody eats eggs. You can't just— They're harmless. Classical French cuisine would be impossible without the egg. All good Europeans eat them. About cholesterol we know so very very little. So-called dietic science is based on exaggeration and innuendo—"

"Nothing to do with dieting, I'm sorry to say," said Hywl, using the enraging smug mock-bashful self-assertion with which people confess to allergies and phobias. "I get migraines."

"But is that so very bad? After all, we now know that the migraine is close cousin, a junior relative, to epilepsy, which has played such an important part in the artistic and political life of the world since the beginning of recorded history—Julius Caesar, Dostoevsky, I could go on. Hywl, my dear boy, I envy you. To take this burden on yourself voluntarily, to eat eggs in the full consciousness of the visionary state one is deliberately embracing, to experience willingly the shaman's trance, the invasion of the godhead, the apprehension of the infinite, to undertake an adventure which—how about mushrooms on toast?"

"Fine."

"Though of course the loss to you *mon cher* is still very great," I said, smoothly recovering and accelerating away like a police driver after a demonstration skid. I began busying myself about the stove.

"The dual magics of egg chemistry underpin so much of European gastronomy. We're all familiar with Escoffier's dictum: *Qu'est-que c'est la cuisine classique de la France? C'est du beurre, du beurre, et encore du beurre.* One might add: *et aussi les oeufs.* And then there are the egg dishes themselves: *oeufs sur le plat, uova al burro,* scrambled eggs, fried eggs, and the various interpretations and national variations on the omelette: *frittata, tortilla,* both of which in my view tend too much to the dry and rubberized, Danish egg-cake, egg foo yong, the Basque classic *piperade,* as well as the authentic French omelette itself, of which my brother was so fond—and which was, indeed, what we ate at our last meal together."

Laura: "Tell me about that. Hugh won't mind."

I turned down the gas slightly.

"Autumn in Norfolk can have a quality of absolute melancholy, of isolation. The year's sap is shrinking, the leaves are sere, one's heart is tugged downwards like a barometer in lowering weather. Et cetera. We overlapped at the cottage, something we didn't often tend to do, for a day and a night, and then in the morning I cooked breakfast, the same thing you're having today (and washed up incidentally, that not being one of Bartholomew's strong points), and then drove down to London and then, the next day, down to here. I was here when he died and of course there's no phone so I found out through a telegram from his penultimate wife. There you are—now I've deliberately gone easy on the salt but I won't feel at all insulted if you'd like a little bit more as I'm acknowledged to have an unsalt tooth, though of course the more one sweats the more salt one is likely to need as I'm sure Hywl will have noticed. An extra twist of pepper to cut the starchiness of the toast for your husband. You'll notice in the middle of the omelette that the egg yolks have just set but are still moist. The trick is not to overload the omelette with filling—confine the actual content of the omelette to a tablespoon or so. There are analogies with other arts if we may for a moment be permitted to sneak in a form/content distinction. Melt the butter over high heat and wait for the foam to subside. Keep the pan hot, and add the filling when the center is beginning to coagulate. Eat, eat."

Amanita phalloides is, in the technical language of mycology, an occasional species—not common, not rare. It has an ammoniacal, sweet, faintly unwholesome smell at close range and is said to have a pleasant, mild, nutty flavor, closer to that of the Shaggy Ink Cap (*Coprinus comatus*) than to the chanterelle (*Cantharellus cibarius*). This flavorsomeness is, to students of fungi, noteworthy, since the overwhelming majority of poisonous mushrooms signal their toxicity by being nasty to smell or eat. So the agreeable taste of *Amanita phalloides* is a good joke on nature's part, since the mushroom is very poisonous indeed—the most poisonous, in fact, in the world, and fully deserving of its common name, the Death Cap (though my own personal favorite name for a lethal fungus belongs to *A. phalloides'* close relative the *Amanita virosa*, or Destroying Angel). *A. phalloides* kills more Continental Europeans than it does Britons, with the Germans having a notably high incidence of mortality— though patriots should note that the first people to be successfully treated for full-blown Death Cap poisoning were a British couple who ate *A. phalloides* in Guernsey in 1973 but were rescued by a doctor's impromptu invention of a blood-filtering technique at London's famous King's College Hospital. The traditional French treatment, or perhaps that should be "treatment," for Death Cap poisoning is to eat large quantities of raw minced rabbit brains. This folk practice is based on the fact that rabbits are immune to the mushroom.

A. phalloides has a liking for deciduous woodland and a particular affinity for oak. It has no especially memorable distinguishing characteristics though it is at the same time not so close in appearance to any desirable mushroom variety to risk being picked and eaten in its stead. (The closest look-alike, *Amanita citrina*, or the False Death Cap, although technically speaking edible, doesn't have much of a culinary following, for obvious reasons. They order these things differently in Japan.) Its cap, between six and twelve centimeters across, convex then expanding, is a not markedly pleasing shade of olive green. The stem, white, is between eight and fifteen centimeters tall, with a ring on the top and a bag-like, sack-like volva almost always attached to the bottom. The toadstool's season—as the distinction between mushroom and toadstool has no scientific force, I use the term here merely as an example of what Fowler sarcastically calls "elegant variation"—is from July to November. In England it is, like many other things, increasingly less common the farther north you go.

The most famous victim of the Death Cap was the Emperor Claudius. He succumbed to a dish of what he thought was *Amanita caesarea,* Caesar's Mushroom, a particularly scrumptious member of the otherwise highly dangerous *Amanita* clan (another first-rate joke on nature's part: the shy beauty in a family of hoodlums). But Claudius's *Amanita caesarea* had been spiked, almost certainly by his wife Agrippina, with an admixture of its fatal cousin—a member of his family poisoning him with a member of the family of what he thought he was eating. "He fell into a coma but vomited up the entire contents of his overloaded stomach and was then poisoned a second time," writes Suetonius, who betrays a forgivable lack of familiarity with the symptoms of Death Cap poisoning. Actually the onset of *A. phalloides* poisoning is almost always followed by a lull and by apparent recovery—victims are discharged from hospital, given a clean bill of health and sent home, and then die several days later. The typical sequence is an intense period of vomiting, diarrhea, and stomach cramps, accompanied by other symptoms such as pronounced anxiety, sweating, and bodily tremors, commencing between six and eight hours after the ingestion of the fungi, and lasting for anything up to forty-eight hours. By the time these symptoms have commenced the greater part of the tissue damage inflicted by *A. phalloides* has already been done. There are two principal toxins involved: one of the peculiarities of fungus poisoning, leading to the extreme difficulty of correct medical diagnosis (before the postmortem stage, when it becomes far more straightforward), is that the toxins combine and recombine with the chemistry of the body and present often insoluble problems of identification. (In the case of *A. phalloides,* of course, there is anyway no antidote.) The two compounds involved in *A. phalloides* poisoning are the amotoxins and the phallotoxins, of which the former seem to be far the most dangerous—phallotoxins are usually broken down in the processes of cooking or digestion. The principal poison is alpha-amotoxin, which acts on RNA in the liver cells to block protein synthesis, thus leading to the death of all those very cells; beta-amotoxin then attacks the tubules of the kidneys before being reabsorbed into the bloodstream (rather than excreted through the urine, which is what ought to happen) to repeat the process; in other words the body is forced to collaborate in the continuing process of poisoning itself. Thus the manifest symptoms are a period of acute stomach upset, as mentioned above, an apparent recovery, and then sudden collapse and death. The cause of death almost always becomes clear during autopsy; after all, it's not every toxin which causes such irrefutably complete hepatic catastrophe. A single mushroom can kill a hearty adult and while exact mortality rates are hard to calibrate and precise figures about dosages are naturally elusive, the approximate fatality rate for *A. phalloides* poisoning would appear to be comfortably above ninety percent.

"Did you go back for the inquest?" asked Laura.

"It was the same coroner as it had been at my parents'. He thanked me for having made the journey—I flew back from Marseille, not my favorite airport, to be frank. Bartholomew appeared to have accidentally poisoned himself: he had a stomach upset on the Monday I left, saw the doctor on Tuesday morning, felt better and then more or less dropped dead on Friday."

"Did he know anything about mushrooms? Was it usual for him to go picking fungi?"

"I blame myself. I know so much more than he did and I would never have picked the relevant fungus by mistake."

"That was delicious," said quick-eating Hywl, using an adjective which, you will have noticed, I have at no point permitted myself in the course of these gastro-historico-psycho-autobiographico-anthropico-philosophic lucubrations.

"Thank you. Help yourself to croissants and confiture. The drive can be taxing as the roads around the Lubéron hills are windy and are sometimes the setting for spectacular thunderstorms, downpours, that sort of thing."

Laura had eaten two-thirds of her omelette and was starting to slow down. She gave her husband a nuptial look which clearly said: Go off and pack, fatty. Hywl rose and wiped his toasty lips on one of my linen napkins, mumbling compliments and apologies as he did so, before trudging upstairs.

"What did you talk about? The last time, with your brother."

"There's a line of Donne's which I often think of, Laura, when I remember our first meeting. 'By our first strange and fatal interview.' In one of the elegies. No—my last conversation with Bartholomew. We talked about the difference between the two most important cultural figures in the modern world, the artist and the murderer. I said that one of the impulses which underlies all art is the desire to make a permanent impact on the world, to leave a trace of selfhood behind. The Sistine Chapel ceiling declares lots of things but one of them is the simple statement *Michelangelo Was Here.* It is one of art's most basic functions, shared by a youth carving his initials into a park bench as well as by Henry Moore leaving those dreary blobs of his all over the place or by Leonardo or whomever—though since I mention him Leonardo could have done with a bit more desire to make a permanent impression or he wouldn't have wasted his time painting frescoes on unfixable surfaces and designing unbuildable flying machines. However, the artist's desire to leave a memento of himself is as directly comprehensible as a dog's action in urinating on a tree. The murderer, though, is better adapted to the reality and to the aesthetics of the modern world, because instead of leaving a presence behind him—the achieved work, whether in the form of a painting or a book or a daubed signature—he leaves behind him something just as final and just as achieved: an absence. Where somebody used to be, now nobody is. What more irrefutable proof of one's having lived can there be than to have taken a human life and replaced it with nothingness, with a few fading memories? To take a stone, throw it into the pond, and ensure that it casts no ripple—surely that's more of an achievement than any, say, of my brother's?

"I said secondly that underlying the artist's disinterestedness, his creation of an abstract and impersonal artifact, lies a brutal determination to assert the self. If the artist's first desire is to leave something behind him, his next is simply to take up more space—to earn a disproportionate amount of the world's attention. This is routinely called 'ego,' but that term is far too mundane to encompass the raging, megalomaniacal desire, the greed, the human deficiency that underpins the creation of everything from a Matisse papercut to a Fabergé egg. Hitler a failed painter, Mao a failed poet; the same urges underlay their earlier and their later careers; but we're so used to this boring perception that we fail to see its true meaning, which is not that the megalomaniac is a failed artist but that the artist is a timid megalomaniac, venting himself in the easy sphere of fantasy rather than the unforgiving arena of real life—Kandinsky a failed Stalin, Klee a Barbie manqué. Why don't people take Bakunin more seriously? Destruction *is* as great a passion as creation, and it is as creative, too—as visionary and as assertive of the self. The artist is the oyster but the murderer is the pearl.

"Then I said what follows from that and what all artists know, that what they give to their creation and to the world can never be matched by the world's response. The inward, solitary, monstrous labor of creation makes the artist feel as if he has *earned* the universe's attention, *earned* its love. But the world isn't interested—it's too busy being the world to do more than vouchsafe the occasional glimpse of its approval, its interest. The adulation of a group of admirers here, the gift of a patron there, prizes and the regard of an audience—these can never have the effect intended, never requite the artist's fundamental demand, which is for simple, universal, unqualified adoration. The artist says to the cosmos: All I ask is infinite love—is that so very wrong? And the cosmos doesn't even bother to respond. The cosmos is photosynthesis, interstellar dust clouds, bus timetables, prison riots, *pi* and *e* and cloud formations. No artist who has ever lived in the history of the world has ever felt adequately attended to for his labors. End result: rage, resentment, bitterness. Who built the country house in Yeats's poem? 'Bitter, violent men.' Quite right. And who expresses, who represents, this bitterness better, the artist or the killer? Merely to ask the question is to answer it.

"And another unanswerable truth: Who can deny that murder is the defining act of our century, as other centuries might have been defined by prayer or mendicancy? Who can put hand on heart and say that the characteristic gesture of the twentieth century is not that of one person killing another? Fifty million dead in the Second World War alone, not to mention the Great War and all the other wars, civil and international, manmade famines, individual killings, spouse-murderings, killings of strangers, revenge killings, race killings, the murders we commit all the time, the murder we are committing even as we sit here, of indifference to those being murdered, I could go on. Every murder contains within itself all murder; each individual act that takes another person's life is the microcosm of our century, as well as another death to add to the total. How can any work of art compete with that, or speak to it, or dare to exist in the face of it at all?

"And then one must also face the sheer naturalness of murder, the unnaturalness of art. Paintings and music, books—they're so arbitrary, so overcomplicated, so full of invention and untruth, compared with the simple human act of taking a life because you don't want someone to carry on existing. There are occasional glimpses of an understanding of this in the world's history. During wartime for example the naturalness of killing is nurtured, encouraged, praised, cultivated—understood. But there are other glimpses, too. Under the *Code Napoléon,* to murder a nagging spouse when the mistral had been blowing for more than seven days was not to be considered a capital crime. That implies, thrillingly, an understanding that the murder of a spouse is sometimes to be, if not actively condoned, then comprehended, allowed for, explained, empathized with—in other words it is to understand that the murder is in some sense natural. As Confucius says, under some circumstances murder can be forgiven; but unreasonableness never is. And what could be more reasonable than to permit oneself to act on one's own impulses? What act is more authentically *human* than murder? Surely not the contortings and strenuosities of the self-appointed priesthood of art, whose attempts at permanence and objectivity and making are at their core a kind of denial of our common humanity. In the Rome of the Caesars, when human nature was allowed fully to flourish and to find unfettered self-expression, murder was endemic—Augustus being poisoned by Livia, who murdered her nephew Germanicus, her sisters, and anyone else who crossed her path; Tiberius doing very similar; Caligula raping and murdering at will; Claudius being poisoned by his wife Agrippina. That's the reality of human nature.

"Besides, the distinction between deed and thought is ludicrously exaggerated in our culture. Christ was right: If you look at a woman with lust you have committed adultery. If you take murder into your heart you have committed it; anyone who has ever harbored a murderous impulse is close, so very close, to the act itself; there is only the thinness of a cigarette paper between the action and the idea—and perhaps, since science tells us that experiences in dreams are, in terms of brain chemistry, as 'real' as events outside them, perhaps anyone who has ever had a thought of murder has in a real sense perpetrated it. This is understood in all tyrannical regimes, where people are murdered not just for plotting against the tyrant but for thinking about plots, or for looking as if they might be about to. All tyrants know that they must kill, not just rebellion, but the idea of rebellion; even the possibility of the idea. To kill hope and the image of hope. No work of art has taken us as far into the heart of man as this. And everybody murders their parents anyway. It's a fact so obvious nobody wants to admit it. We outlive them, we surpass them; we murder them by our simplest happiness. And if we don't, then they have murdered us. There, I said to Bartholomew, have I given you enough reasons?"

Hywl had been standing in the kitchen doorway for I don't know how long, the familiar-to-me pair of honeymoon suitcases stiffly distributed between his plump red hands. He was holding the bags off the ground as if to set them down would cause an explosion. He importantly said:

"Time to be off, darling."

"What did your brother say?" asked Laura.

"He said: 'Reasons for what?' "

We embarked on the banality of partings. Farewells and separations never, I find, quite live up to the drama they promise to afford. Human beings (I find again) have a tendency to feel the wrong quantity of emotion, or indeed the wrong emotion, so that life is an endless process of liquid being poured into and exchanged between badly designed containers, the wrong color, the wrong shape, the wrong size. Of all human talents the most evenly shared is the gift of incongruity. At my brother's funeral a gusting Norfolk wind kept bringing us chunks of football commentary from the garden of the building which used to be the vicar's house; now he lived in a flat in our market town and the former vicarage belonged to a hard-golfing Norwich solicitor and his quasi-delinquent teenage sons. As I stood at the graveside (my brother's celebrity having compelled or seduced the vicar into allowing him to be buried in a full coffin in a graveyard that was officially "full" and accessible only for the interment of ashes, so that this burial became a cause of some controversy and good solid Norfolk *ressentiment*), elegant in a freshly purchased black suit (the outfit bought in conscious defiance of Thoreau's maxim to beware of any enterprise requiring new clothes—on the contrary one should maximize all efforts to seek them out!), preparing to drop a single black orchid onto Bartholomew's coffin, various toadies, apparatchiks, journalists, and ex-wives behind me vying for the privilege of adding their handful of earth, as I stood there the football commentary reached a new pitch of male hysteria, a climax of excited imbecilism, as the Oafs revenged last year's defeat at the hands of the Morons, and as the flower, ordered two days in advance from Wyckham's the Florists, dropped from my manicured fingers.

My parting with Laura and Hywl did not scale/plumb the same heights/depths but was more Englishly unsatisfactory. Hywl loaded the bags into the back of the tinny hired Fiat while Laura and I stood in front of each other as if we were formally inviting each other to dance. To touch or not to touch. Hywl came around and blokishly shook my hand, his grip predictably overemphatic, before tactfully retreating and levering himself into the passenger's seat. Laura and I moved toward each other and at the same moment, with the same combination of deliberation yielding to overhaste, so that our noses just avoided brushing, we exchanged a kiss, the innermost section of which just involved each other's lips; hers were unexpectedly dry.

"Thank you so very much," she said.

"Don't thank me."

And then she was in the car, busily adjusting the seat and the mirror before strapping herself in in one crisp movement. She started the engine and wound down the window.

"Thanks again."

I said nothing but merely raised my hand in a benediction and wave, and kept it there as she tidily reversed the car out of the gate before heading off down the lane toward the village, her husband with his head bent in some nausea-inducing feat of map consultation. I stood by the gate with my hand still aloft and watched them go down the track, a smoking contrail of grit rising in their wake. In a moment they would pass the projected and hotly controversial location for the new municipal dump. Do you know the feeling, when you've eaten half a biscuit and put the rest down somewhere, and now you can't remember where, so that you're left with a sense of incompleteness, of unfinished business, of an itch you can't scratch? And then there's the other feeling, when you've done something unclean, something polluting or excremental, with your hands, and you haven't had time to wash them yet, and you have to think back hard and even so you still can't quite remember what happened to make you feel besmirched, and the only certainty you have now is something to do with a lingering taint. I turned and walked back up to the house. By the time I got there the murdered couple had gone around the corner onto the main road, leaving behind them a slow cloud of settling dust.